DEATH

IN

FLORENCE

(A Year in Europe—Book 2)

BLAKE PIERCE

Blake Pierce

Blake Pierce is the USA Today bestselling author of the RILEY PAGE mystery series, which includes seventeen books. Blake Pierce is also the author of the MACKENZIE WHITE mystery series, comprising fourteen books; of the AVERY BLACK mystery series, comprising six books; of the KERI LOCKE mystery series, comprising five books; of the MAKING OF RILEY PAIGE mystery series, comprising six books; of the KATE WISE mystery series, comprising seven books; of the CHLOE FINE psychological suspense mystery, comprising six books; of the JESSE HUNT psychological suspense thriller series, comprising fifteen books (and counting); of the AU PAIR psychological suspense thriller series, comprising three books; of the ZOE PRIME mystery series, comprising six books; of the ADELE SHARP mystery series, comprising ten books (and counting); of the EUROPEAN VOYAGE cozy mystery series, comprising six books (and counting); of the new LAURA FROST FBI suspense thriller, comprising three books (and counting); of the new ELLA DARK FBI suspense thriller, comprising six books (and counting); of the A YEAR IN EUROPE cozy mystery series, comprising three books (and counting); of the AVA GOLD mystery series, comprising three books (and counting); and of the RACHEL GIFT mystery series, comprising three books (and counting).

An avid reader and lifelong fan of the mystery and thriller genres, Blake loves to hear from you, so please feel free to visit www.blakepierceauthor.com to learn more and stay in touch.

LEFT TO RUN (Book #2)
LEFT TO HIDE (Book #3)
LEFT TO KILL (Book #4)
LEFT TO MURDER (Book #5)
LEFT TO ENVY (Book #6)
LEFT TO LAPSE (Book #7)
LEFT TO VANISH (Book #8)
LEFT TO HUNT (Book #9)
LEFT TO FEAR (Book #10)

THE AU PAIR SERIES
ALMOST GONE (Book#1)
ALMOST LOST (Book #2)
ALMOST DEAD (Book #3)

ZOE PRIME MYSTERY SERIES
FACE OF DEATH (Book#1)
FACE OF MURDER (Book #2)
FACE OF FEAR (Book #3)
FACE OF MADNESS (Book #4)
FACE OF FURY (Book #5)
FACE OF DARKNESS (Book #6)

A JESSIE HUNT PSYCHOLOGICAL SUSPENSE SERIES
THE PERFECT WIFE (Book #1)
THE PERFECT BLOCK (Book #2)
THE PERFECT HOUSE (Book #3)
THE PERFECT SMILE (Book #4)
THE PERFECT LIE (Book #5)
THE PERFECT LOOK (Book #6)
THE PERFECT AFFAIR (Book #7)
THE PERFECT ALIBI (Book #8)
THE PERFECT NEIGHBOR (Book #9)
THE PERFECT DISGUISE (Book #10)
THE PERFECT SECRET (Book #11)
THE PERFECT FAÇADE (Book #12)
THE PERFECT IMPRESSION (Book #13)
THE PERFECT DECEIT (Book #14)
THE PERFECT MISTRESS (Book #15)

CHLOE FINE PSYCHOLOGICAL SUSPENSE SERIES

NEXT DOOR (Book #1)
A NEIGHBOR'S LIE (Book #2)
CUL DE SAC (Book #3)
SILENT NEIGHBOR (Book #4)
HOMECOMING (Book #5)
TINTED WINDOWS (Book #6)

KATE WISE MYSTERY SERIES
IF SHE KNEW (Book #1)
IF SHE SAW (Book #2)
IF SHE RAN (Book #3)
IF SHE HID (Book #4)
IF SHE FLED (Book #5)
IF SHE FEARED (Book #6)
IF SHE HEARD (Book #7)

THE MAKING OF RILEY PAIGE SERIES
WATCHING (Book #1)
WAITING (Book #2)
LURING (Book #3)
TAKING (Book #4)
STALKING (Book #5)
KILLING (Book #6)

RILEY PAIGE MYSTERY SERIES
ONCE GONE (Book #1)
ONCE TAKEN (Book #2)
ONCE CRAVED (Book #3)
ONCE LURED (Book #4)
ONCE HUNTED (Book #5)
ONCE PINED (Book #6)
ONCE FORSAKEN (Book #7)
ONCE COLD (Book #8)
ONCE STALKED (Book #9)
ONCE LOST (Book #10)
ONCE BURIED (Book #11)
ONCE BOUND (Book #12)
ONCE TRAPPED (Book #13)
ONCE DORMANT (Book #14)
ONCE SHUNNED (Book #15)
ONCE MISSED (Book #16)

ONCE CHOSEN (Book #17)

MACKENZIE WHITE MYSTERY SERIES
BEFORE HE KILLS (Book #1)
BEFORE HE SEES (Book #2)
BEFORE HE COVETS (Book #3)
BEFORE HE TAKES (Book #4)
BEFORE HE NEEDS (Book #5)
BEFORE HE FEELS (Book #6)
BEFORE HE SINS (Book #7)
BEFORE HE HUNTS (Book #8)
BEFORE HE PREYS (Book #9)
BEFORE HE LONGS (Book #10)
BEFORE HE LAPSES (Book #11)
BEFORE HE ENVIES (Book #12)
BEFORE HE STALKS (Book #13)
BEFORE HE HARMS (Book #14)

AVERY BLACK MYSTERY SERIES
CAUSE TO KILL (Book #1)
CAUSE TO RUN (Book #2)
CAUSE TO HIDE (Book #3)
CAUSE TO FEAR (Book #4)
CAUSE TO SAVE (Book #5)
CAUSE TO DREAD (Book #6)

KERI LOCKE MYSTERY SERIES
A TRACE OF DEATH (Book #1)
A TRACE OF MUDER (Book #2)
A TRACE OF VICE (Book #3)
A TRACE OF CRIME (Book #4)
A TRACE OF HOPE (Book #5)

CHAPTER ONE

Florence.

Even when Diana was a little girl, the name of the Italian town had inspired thoughts of lush landscapes, cobblestone streets, flowery breezes, and romance.

Lots of romance.

So it was ironic that Diana was here, in Italy, on her whirlwind European trip—completely alone.

Diana had always been a planner, detailing things almost down to the minute. But when she'd left Paris, she'd made a decision. She'd spent the ten-hour high-speed bullet train ride (with a transfer in Milan) transforming her itinerary, which was once full of sites and excursions every tourist wanted to see, to something else.

A bucket list, of sorts, personalized to her.

The first item on the list? *Fall in love in Italy.*

A tall order, considering she couldn't speak the language, was newly divorced and had been hurt before, and wasn't exactly a spring chicken.

But as she stepped off the train at Firenze Santa Maria Novella railway station early that morning, she dragged in a bracing breath of chilly air and smiled, excited by the challenge. She looked around at the many tourists scurrying about like mice, energized and thrilling over the possibilities.

I can do this. And it's going to be great.

Smiling from ear to ear, she retrieved her luggage and walked along the concourse, listening to the musical sound of the Italian language wafting up from the intercom and from people around her. In the background, Andrea Bocelli crooned. The rich scent of roast coffee and vanilla coming from a tiny *pasticceria* tantalized her. The station was modern and nondescript, a boxy warehouse by American standards, but a little shiver went through her as she stepped outside into the warm light of morning and gazed up at the Italian flag flapping in the breeze, and the tile-roofed Florence buildings scattered about the hillside.

She stepped around a rack, brimming with bicycles, and stood in front of the McDonald's (a reminder that she could never fully escape America, no matter how hard she tried), waiting for a taxi. She decided to wait to check her phone for messages, which she was sure would all be from Lily and Bea, her adult children in vastly different time zones, and all of them versions of *Are you okay?*

They hadn't believed she could do this. Didn't think she'd make it. Thought she'd come back after the first week.

But she'd muddled through. Paris had been an adventure, what with nearly being arrested and murdered. No, it hadn't been everything she was hoping for. Far from it. But in a lot of ways, it'd been more.

And she already couldn't wait to see what kind of adventure she'd find in Italy.

A taxi pulled up at the curb, and an old man popped out, smiling at her as he tipped his flat cap and took her luggage. *"Buongiorno."*

"Buongiorno!" she replied, scrolling through the translation app on her phone. "Um . . . *Per favore portami a questo indirizzo . . . Castello Di Gabbiano?"* Could you please take me to this address?

"Ah. Si," he said, opening the door for her and helping her in. Then he slipped into the driver's seat, and they took off into the wondrous historic city nestled in the heart of Tuscany.

The city proper was full of small, winding streets that it seemed the small cab would barely fit through. Though much of it was like any ordinary city, with streets full of busy, fashionable people, tightly packed modern buildings, and traffic, everywhere around were signs of the rich history of this part of the world. She kept her eyes peeled for the unique sights that made Florence *Florence*, looking for things that had been on her *old* list, the Cathedral of Santa Maria, the Galleria, and more. She still planned to see them, but since all her plans in Paris had been thrown into the air and she'd still had an amazing time, she'd decided to be more flexible about it.

Not exactly an easy thing. After fifty-two years of rigid scheduling, this leopard wasn't going to change its spots overnight. Still, she was determined, and as a former successful businesswoman who'd clawed her way up the corporate ladder, she was used to facing adversity head-on, and adapting, if necessary.

She gazed in awe as they swung around a corner and the brick-red dome of the massive Cathedral of Santa Maria appeared in the window, framed by a gorgeous pink sunrise. Slowly, the pink and green façade of the architectural marvel came into view, the sunlight gleaming off of its many intricate windows, its white, green, and red marble surface, and the bronze ball atop the cupola, which, she'd read, had been soldered by none other than Leonardo DaVinci himself. She shivered a bit at the thought, at the feeling of being in the presence of such a magnificent piece of history.

The taxi sailed on past the cathedral, past many other buildings, spaced farther and farther apart, most with stucco facades and burnt orange terracotta roofs. They came out to a valley, with rolling hills and a vineyard stretching below, with rows and rows of grapevines baking in the sun. The driver pointed at a large stone building in the distance with an impressive tower and a medieval turret, just like the kind a princess would gaze out from.

Her hotel. A castle.

She'd planned to play it by ear, but on the train ride, she'd stumbled upon this place on her phone and couldn't resist. An old castle amidst a vineyard, full of rooms with canopy beds and stone floors and views of the rolling green countryside? Yes, please! After seeing it, she'd added it to her itinerary. *Stay in a medieval castle.*

Now, she was really glad she'd booked in for three nights. The place was even better than the pictures she'd seen on TripAdvisor.

The cab pulled up a brick drive and drove through stone arches climbing with vines before stopping under a rustic wooden portico. By then, it was far too warm for a jacket, so she slipped it off and tied it around her waist. As she stepped out, two handsome young valets rushed to her service, fussing to help her with her one bag. They spoke in rapid-fire Italian, ushering her on into the lobby. Though stone-walled, it was by no means a cold space. In fact, with the sun pouring in the open windows and a large ceiling made entirely of stained glass, it was warm and inviting. There were wine kegs stacked in a corner, and rustic bottles placed on almost every surface. *The home of Chianti.* That's what the website had said.

As she stood there, fumbling with her wallet for her credit card, she heard someone giggle. She looked up to see a young blonde woman pulling her considerably older lover along with her, toward a light-filled patio. He had a stupid grin under his salt-and-pepper moustache.

Of course, Diana thought of Evan, her ex, who'd traded Diana in for his own younger, blonder model, whom Diana and her girls referred

3

to, not-so-affectionately, as Vidal, since all of her substance was in her hair.

Shoving those thoughts away, she pulled out her MasterCard and was just about to approach the reception desk when the elevator doors opened, and out stepped a young, starry-eyed couple, arms wrapped tightly around each other. They kissed as they walked, nearly bumping into Diana as she stood there.

"Oh. Um, sorry," the young, goateed guy said in an American accent, confused to find her there. Before she could respond, he was locking lips again with his companion and heading out the doors.

"No problem," Diana murmured. As she turned to head to the desk, a couple jumped in line in front of her, speaking German and throwing their massive backpacks on the ground. They were scruffy, the man with an unkempt beard and the woman with bits of dried leaves in her hair, both in hiking boots and shorts. Diana wondered if they'd just hiked over the Alps to arrive here.

They retrieved their key and, hand in hand, headed toward the elevator.

Diana watched them go, a sinking feeling in her stomach.

Italy was for lovers. She knew that.

But still . . . why did it seem like the Universe was rubbing it in her face?

Who cared if it was morning? She needed a glass of Chianti, stat. *Like the girls in the office used to say, it's five o'clock somewhere.*

Shrugging it off, she stepped up to the counter, patted her chest, and said, "St. James. *Prenotazione*," which she'd been practicing in her head while on the train. *St. James. Reservation.*

The pert, fairy-like woman behind the counter smiled. "Ah, Signora St. James. We are very happy to welcome you to our place. I trust you have had a good trip here?"

English. Thank goodness, Diana thought as the woman typed something into her computer. "Yes. Thank you. Is there a place I can go for breakfast?"

The clerk nodded and pointed to some double doors, from where the faint sound of conversation and clinking silverware and dishes emanated. "We're serving right now."

With that, Diana's stomach growled. She hadn't eaten anything since a croissant in Paris, right before she'd boarded the train. She was starving.

4

"Thank you," she said, taking her key card from the clerk. "I mean, *grazie*."

"You're very welcome. Enjoy your stay with us."

Diana headed for the elevator, smiling. *I'm sure I will. Now, time to freshen up and change before breakfast and touring the grounds.*

She walked down a dark, travertine-tiled hallway until she found her room. Pushing open the heavy wooden door, she gasped. The room had a high ceiling, crossed with rafters, and the space was simply enormous, so much so that the canopied queen bed, draped in organza curtains, was practically dwarfed by its size. Sunshine spilled in through a massive, open bay window.

Crossing to it, Diana peered outside at the rolling hills, and the rows of grape plants, lined against the lush green valley, cut by a single dirt path. Off to the side was a crystal clear pool with waterfall, fashioned from river stone, surrounded by umbrellaed tables. The sky was blue and cloudless, and the air smelled of earth, honey, and fruit.

"I have to take a picture of this," she said aloud, feeling in her purse for her phone. No, she wasn't one for selfies, but this scene before her simply demanded it.

She dipped her hand in her enormous purse, coming up empty. Then she felt for her pockets, before she realized the travel outfit she was wearing didn't *have* pockets.

She checked her purse again, more frantically now, the hair on her neck rising to full attention as she confirmed her suspicion.

No no no no no, her mind screamed as she looked around, helpless for some indication of where she could look next. But there was no other place. She'd used it on the train, in the taxi . . . hadn't she? She couldn't remember. Her mind spun with half-formed thoughts, and from these, one irrefutable fact rose above all others.

Her phone was gone.

CHAPTER TWO

Gone. Just gone.

Diana shuddered at the thought of her precious iPhone, in the hands of some thug who'd look at her photos and private information, intruding on her life. She had *everything* on that phone, her whole entire being. Maybe he'd even use it to commit crimes in her name and get her into just as much trouble as she'd been in in Paris.

And now, what was she going to do? As she stood in line in a busy electronics store, she ripped her thumbnail off in her anxiety and peered down at the ragged remnants of it. She needed to stop that.

Instinctively, for the thousandth time that hour, she reached into her purse for her phone.

Bzzzzz. Sorry.

Only now that it was missing did Diana realize what it had been to her. No, she wasn't as attached to her phone as her children were, but over the years, it'd come to be her security blanket. It was especially so now, where she didn't know the language or the landscape. Standing here, in a strange country, she felt farther away from the United States than ever. She shivered again, feeling exposed to attack. Naked.

It'd been a struggle just getting this far. When she'd first realized it was gone, she'd hurried downstairs, hoping to find it in the reception area. No such luck. Then she'd retraced her steps out to the curb, where the two valets helped her look for it. Nothing.

The clerk helped her make a call to her wireless provider, who explained that out of the country, there was nothing they could do to replace a lost cell phone. After a good amount of freaking out and, yes, a lot of gnashed teeth, the clerk offered to put her in a taxi to the nearest iPhone store, FastWeb Cellular, in downtown Florence.

Now, as she stood in line, cataloging everything that she'd be missing without her phone, her stomach sank more and more. Her contacts were gone. Sadly, she didn't even know the phone numbers of her own daughters, since she was so used to speed-dialing them. She had no method of taking or keeping any photographs of the marvelous things she'd see—so she'd probably forget half of this trip. And forget about touring—without the opening and closing times of museums, she'd be a lost puppy. How would she be able to pick a restaurant without checking the menus online first? And without the hourly weather forecast . . . what if it rained?

Calm down, Diana. You're five minutes away from buying a new cell phone. You can handle this momentary blip.

She stepped up to the counter. "*Buongiorno.* I'd like an iPhone."

The man nodded and handed her a tablet. "Fill this out. You get in a week."

"A week? But—"

"New iPhones are on backorder. Could be sooner. You give us number, we call when they come in, *si?*"

She filled out the form. "Is there a way I can get a phone to use right now?"

He looked at her like she was insane. "Not here. We all cleaned out. Try next door."

After finishing there, she went to the next shop over. The place wasn't exactly an Apple Store, something Diana had noticed the moment she'd stepped inside. Aside from that it didn't appear to have any cases or displays with the latest gadgets, it also sold old appliances, like space heaters and box television sets. There was a partially bald cat sitting in the window, under a neon sign that said *Elettronica.* Diana had to wonder if the clerk had made a mistake. She hadn't lost her toaster oven; she'd lost her phone.

As the person in line in front of her stepped away from the counter with a new-to-them electric kettle, Diana attacked it, a feverish heat flushing her face. "Hello, I, um—"

She winced when the old lady in the housecoat behind the counter stared at her, unamused. That was another thing. No phone, no easy translations.

Taking a breath, she tried again. "*Ciao.* I'm looking for . . ." She made her hands into binoculars, cupping them around her eyes. Then put a pinky and thumb to her cheek. "Phone?"

"Ah, *telefono.*"

The woman reached behind the counter and pulled out an old, rotary-dial phone from Diana's youth, circa 1968.

"No. A cell phone? You know, newer?"

"*Cellulare?*" The woman nodded. "*Si?*"

"Yes. Right. *Si?* Do you have?"

Again, the woman nodded and shuffled into the back room. When she returned, the old lady was using the hem of her housecoat to polish something, lifting it up to bare her doughy white legs. When she set it on the counter, Diana winced.

It was an old flip phone, circa the turn of the century. Diana had had one of those . . . once. Back in the olden days, those and BlackBerries were high-tech.

At least it wasn't the size of her forearm, but still . . . what kind of features did something like that have? The sinking feeling turned to outright nausea. This was bad. Really bad. "You don't have anything newer?"

The woman stared at her, uncomprehending.

She didn't have time for this. Besides, something was better than nothing. "Fine. Can you hook that up to my service so that I can get it to work?"

Again, the woman stared. Diana's shoulders slumped, and she was ready to call it a day, when a voice in the back said, "I can."

A younger man with a full head of dark hair and a tan came out of the back, picking up the phone. "You're American, yes?"

She nodded as he looked her over, feeling herself blushing. He was probably about her height, a good six inches shorter than Evan, and yet he had the face of a movie star, the only signs of age a few creases at the corners of his eyes. Her breath caught.

"Lost your phone, eh?"

"Yes."

He picked up the cell phone and inspected it. "You'll need a SIM card from the carrier but I can get you set up. Usually, we don't get people wanting new cell phones around here. Especially with FastWeb Cellular right down the street."

"Oh—" She looked around. She knew she had to have been taken to the wrong place. As she wondered if it would be impolite to tell him no thanks, he spoke again.

"But you know what, I think these little babies have something special to them that the new phones don't. People these days are too into their phones. They don't look around to see what is going on." He held up the flip phone. "This is just what it's supposed to be. A phone. That's all."

Just what it's supposed to be. Right. A phone. Not a lifeline.

She'd gone on this trip to assert her independence. To learn the ancient art of relying on oneself. What was so independent about being tethered to a piece of electronic equipment?

Besides, the man was right. She'd lived almost half her life without a cell phone, and life had been a lot different then. Freer. More fun. She remembered fondly the days of paper maps, of pulling over to the side of the road to chart a course with a highlighter. It was much more adventurous, exciting, heading out, not knowing every little thing about your destination.

Which was exactly what Diana had attempted to accomplish, first with her itinerary, and now with her phone.

As the man behind the counter worked on the phone, a little chill passed through her. Could she live without a smartphone, using one that was only good to put in the occasional call to her kids?

Maybe.

Was it possible? Well, she guessed she was about to find out.

The man handed her the phone. "You're all set. You remember how to use one like this?"

She stared at it, remembering those days of the early 2000s, when she'd had one just like this. All she'd used it for was phone calls, usually meetings, on her drives into and out of New York City, before driving and talking on cell phones had been outlawed. Nobody texted back then, because texting took forever. Pictures were grainy and terrible. Really, a phone call and voicemail was all it was good for.

And maybe that was just what she needed.

If only she could let herself believe that.

She took it and handed him her credit card. "Thank you. It looks great."

As she turned and walked away from the counter, she noticed a rack with brochures and maps to various local attractions near the door, sandwiched among a dusty eight-track console and an ancient bullet-shaped refrigerator. She lifted out a brochure which included a map of downtown Florence. Yes, this would do very nicely. And, bonus—she didn't have to worry about it running out of charge.

When she stepped outside, she smiled. Really, who cared if it rained when she was out exploring? She'd never melted before. This would be fun. And that was what she'd come to Europe for.

*

9

A few moments later, she walked past the cell phone store again, trying to tell herself that it was only the old Diana who needed an iPhone.

But this was the new Diana. The Diana who rolled with the punches. Who let fate take her around, like a feather on the wind.

As she walked, she came across the Palazzo Vecchio, the town hall of Florence, a square, stone palace with its remarkable high tower stretching into the sky. She stared up at it, gazing at the remarkable architecture, and noticed the statues flanking the front entrance. She nearly tripped over another person, trying to get a better look at the one to the left. Wait . . . was that Michelangelo's *David*? It certainly looked like it, though in pictures, it'd never had quite so much pigeon poop on it.

She looked at the map, then back at it. It was a replica. Turned out, the actual *David* statue was at the Accademia, several blocks northward. The map was written in Italian, but from what she could tell, this *used* to be the spot where the actual statue once stood.

She'd have to get to the Accademia, eventually. But right now, as she studied the map and the location of the nearest attraction, something far more exciting caught her eye . . .

Following the road signs, she traveled down another block, following the Arno River, until it came into view.

Her breath caught.

There it was.

CHAPTER THREE

She nearly tripped on the uneven stone of the old street, so fascinated was she by the sight.

It was the Ponte Vecchio. Tourist trap or not, this esteemed, romantic, thousand-year-old bridge had been on her bucket list since she was a little kid, even since she'd first heard about it in grade school. Once, she'd even imagined her husband-to-be putting a lock on the bridge to profess his love for her, or buying an engagement ring for her at one of the many jewelry shops, dropping to his knee and proposing to her, right on this spot.

But right now, she didn't need any of that. She was just excited to be here, in a place she'd only dreamed about and seen from the screen of her cell phone.

Yes, the man at the electronics store was absolutely right. There was so much out there to see, which couldn't be experienced with a cell phone. This totally beat any experience she could have with her cell. The brightly colored shops, sandwiched together in the center of the Arno, beckoned to her, making her heart do a little dance in her chest. She picked up the pace and fell in line with a large crowd of tourists, all flocking to the area.

In the confines of the narrow bridge, she inhaled the scent of fresh-baked bread and coffee, which had to be better than what it had smelled like in the thirteenth century, when it was nothing but butchers and tanners who took up residence here. It was the Medicis, in the fifteenth century, who moved the silver and goldsmiths into the shops, transforming the area to what it was today, a mecca for shoppers. She looked up at the second floor, which she'd read was now an art gallery. In the Medici era, though, it'd been a secret passage, for the royalty of the Renaissance era to cross the river.

That little piece of history was all so fascinating, but what thrilled her more was actually, finally, after so many years of dreaming . . . *being a part of it.*

She stopped at the first café she came to and bought a cup of espresso and a *sfogliatella*, savoring the light, flaky layers of crust covered in powdered sugar. As she meandered down the street, she noticed people congregating at the statue in the square at the very center of the road, a bust of *Benvenuto Cellini*, the famous goldsmith and sculptor. Though placing locks on the bridge was now illegal, several of them were attached to the iron gate surrounding the sculpture.

Diana supposed that was one way to show one's love for another person—doing something forbidden that could come with a hefty fine.

As she walked closer to the square, licking powdered sugar from her fingers, she peered up at the statue. Funny, he looked a little like Evan, her ex.

But Evan was far too practical to do anything that could get him in trouble. Though she'd wanted all the romance, the locks, the romantic proposal, she'd gotten none of that from him. He'd proposed to her in the kitchen of their first apartment in Brooklyn, on a weekday morning before he left for work. No ring; it'd just been a, "Hey, here's a crazy idea . . ." kind of thing. She'd been wearing his boxer shorts and a T-shirt, and three minutes before that, she'd been sucking down coffee, trying to wake herself up. She hadn't even brushed her teeth.

Good thing selfies *hadn't* existed back then, because it definitely wasn't a film-worthy moment.

She looked up at the windblown locks of Benvenuto Cellini, wondering if he was any more romantic. He looked it; dashing and handsome, with just a bit of a devilishly adventurous side. If he had been here, would he have swept her off her feet? Offered her a lock? Or even just a romantic stroll? A wink and a blown kiss? Anything?

Heck, even simply letting her *be* on this bridge would've been a step up. Though Diana had begged him all of their twenty-eight years of marriage, Evan had always been too busy to take her on that trip to Europe. How many times had she asked him? A billion?

She laughed to herself. Of course it never would've worked out. Of course. Why had it taken her so long to realize that?

A breeze picked up, blowing the salty, cool scent of the Arno over to her, and her stomach fluttered a bit. Like in Paris, it felt a bit magical here. Like dreams could come true. Like the start of a great, world-changing adventure. It had been that, for likely thousands of couples who'd started their happily-ever-after, right here.

As she stood there, she wished she could, in some small way, be a part of the history and time-honored tradition of the bridge.

But how, Diana? Unless you plan on jumping from it. You're alone, remember?

She took another sip of her espresso. When she looked away, she noticed a man staring at her. He was a businessman, with a full head of silver hair, wearing a suit, and sitting at one of the outdoor bistro tables with his legs crossed, an open newspaper on his lap. Older, yes, maybe late fifties, but men always seemed to look better with age. Evan had gotten better looking, too, as much as she hated to admit it. This man was so devastatingly attractive, so perfect, Diana almost looked around to see where the camera crew was, filming him.

Then why was he staring at *her*?

She tried to look away but found she couldn't. His eyes had magnetized her. The man was as fascinating as a train wreck, she thought, and probably as damaging as one, too. Really, Evan had done a number on her heart, making it wither in her chest—there was no reason why she would want to jump back into those dangerous waters again and risk further damaging it. And yet another part of her heart, the part that responded now, throbbed, coming to life, wanting her to dive in, head-first.

She clasped a hand over it to tell it to behave as she looked up and locked eyes with him again. God, he had gorgeous eyes, bright blue, like the sky.

He smiled.

She smiled back coyly.

A little part of her brain tickled with the image of the two of them walking this bridge, arm in arm. Eduardo— he looked like an Eduardo—would of course be wearing that fantastic custom suit, and yet he wouldn't be concerned with anything but her. He'd be so overcome with love that he'd drop to his knee—saying to hell with any stains he might get on the fabric!—pulling out a magnificent diamond ring that sparkled in the Italian sunlight.

As the image solidified in her mind, he winked in a sexy, leisurely way.

Winked! At her? Was this really happening?

Then he blew her a kiss.

She gawked. At that moment, she imagined them together, so in love that nothing around them seemed to matter. "Marry me, my love, and be with me for always," he'd say, both in Italian and English, because one language hardly seemed like enough.

Then, as she covered her mouth and cried softly, he'd slip the ring onto her finger as a crowd of envious onlookers watched. She'd smile through her tears and say, "Of course, of course. I want nothing more."

As this thought settled in her mind, he waved, and his smile grew.

Normally stoic and strong, there'd be tears in his own eyes. "You've made me the happiest man alive," he'd say, reaching into the pocket of that expensive blazer. He'd pull out an old padlock, shaped like a heart, with an intricate brass key, and braving the possibility of arrest or a fine, he'd lock it on the gate, and with all his might, throw the key into the Arno.

Then he'd take her in his arms, kissing her passionately, and—

He suddenly stood up and began to bee-line his way toward her.

Nervousness seeped in, tamping down the dreamy, giddy bubbles inside her, and her throat went dry. She swallowed, trying to keep her breathing calm as he wove his way through the crowd, his eyes still trained on hers.

Diana gripped her coffee for dear life and licked her lips, hoping she didn't have powdered sugar there. *I should say "Ciao." Or "Buongiorno." Or "Ciao"? Is it too late in the day for "Buongiorno"? Help!*

When he was just steps away from her, she blurted, *"Chiorno!"*

Confusion tangled his face and she wanted to crawl into the cracks on the stone floor, but it only lasted a second. Because within that second, his smile returned . . . just long enough so that he could pass by Diana, hurrying toward the raven-haired beauty lounging against the railing of the bridge.

Diana spun to see him wrap an arm around her. They smiled together and shared the romantic kiss she'd been fantasizing about, then gazed out, together, over the Arno.

Diana stood there, pulled the cover off her espresso, and stared into its murky depths. She took a sip and rolled her eyes. "Chiorno. Really, Diana?" she muttered to herself, as a sound rose up over the regular Italian chatter.

A voice said, "Oh, honey, that's perfect," and a familiar laugh greeted her ears.

She knew that laugh, because, well, she'd spent over twenty-eight years listening to it.

No. It couldn't be.

She spun around, sure she had to have been hearing things. It was the shock of the rejection from Eduardo, that was all. Now, the voice of her ex-husband was haunting her. That was it. After all, Evan had just returned from proposing to his too-young girlfriend in Haiti, less than a month ago. He was a busy surgeon, far too busy to go traipsing all over the world. Wasn't that what he told her? *I can't get away, Di. I know you really want to go on vacation, but my practice needs me. Maybe next year.* So she'd sacrificed, for him. For his career. And it had been worth it. He now had a thriving practice and was known as one of the best and most respected surgeons in New York City, which meant that there was absolutely no way that he could be . . .

Right?

But as she looked up at one of the jewelry stores, a tiny place with a glass case right up front advertising *diamanti*, she saw his back, a back she knew just as well as his front—linen shirt, too-long graying hair, the tanned limbs of a man who'd once been an athlete . . . Her stomach dropped, and she confirmed it.

Standing not ten yards away from her was, in part, what she'd left America to escape.

Her ex-husband, Evan.

CHAPTER FOUR

Nope. Not possible.

As she stood there among the beauty that was Florence, staring as her ex-husband browsed the jewelry cases, hand-in-hand with a young, blonde nightmare, Diana was convinced she was seeing things.

She blinked. Blinked harder. Still there. Pinched herself. No change.

All of that failing, she looked around, desperate for a place to escape to. If *they* were here, she certainly didn't want to be, too.

Too late. At that moment, her ex turned around and caught sight of her. The blissful smile painted on his dopey, in-love face morphed to delighted surprise. Diana's cheeks flamed hot as he waved at her.

She groaned under her breath, "Here we go," and plastered her own stupid smile on her face as she walked over. She said, too loudly and far more joyously than she felt, "Fancy meeting you here."

He leaned in for a kiss as his fiancée turned around, her long locks nearly whipping in Diana's face. Diana stiffly completed the cordial act, her skin crawling the whole time. As she moved back, she noticed dark marking, the promise of an inked heart, hiding underneath his partly opened shirt, right near the collarbone.

He'd gotten a tattoo? Probably emblazoned with his intended's name. What happened to his assertion that the body was a temple, and that ink of any sort was like graffiti, dirty and defiling?

She didn't need to look far for the answer. Tilda had quite a few tattoos of her own—some Chinese symbol on her wrist, a smattering of roses on a vine snaking up her ankle. Probably a tramp stamp on her back.

Tilda was, after all, about half his age, and had gone to school with Bea, her youngest. The two hadn't been friends since middle school, when Bea got serious about her studies and Tilda got serious about . . . other things. Bea had nicknamed her Vidal Sassoon, because all of her brains were in her hair. The name fit. The woman had some serious hair, piled atop her head like a macaron tower and spilling over her shoulders. The last time Diana had been this close to Tilda, she'd been doling out cupcakes in the backyard for Bea's eighth birthday. Little had she known that that cute, pigtailed blonde would transform into *this*.

Tilda let out a long giggle that sounded like a cross between a seagull screeching and a car alarm going off. Her jaw dropped wide. "Mrs. St. James! I didn't know you'd be here!" she exclaimed, leaning in and giving her the double-cheek kiss. She smelled like bubblegum, and indeed, that was because she was chewing and popping some. She giggled some more. "Oh. I guess I'm going to be the future Mrs. St. James! Isn't that funny?"

Hilarious. Diana smiled as Tilda extended her fragile hand to reveal a diamond that looked even more expensive than it had the first time Diana had seen it, on Instagram. Expensive and . . . gaudy. Not her style at all.

But, clearly, Vidal's. One only needed to look at her to know that. She was wearing a sunshine-yellow dress that bared far too much skin. It was almost indecent, the way the two yellow triangles up top fought unsuccessfully to keep the young woman's huge breasts covered. They were spilling out over the top and sides, shouting, *Here we are!* Diana didn't have to look around to know that people were staring at her, at them. It was impossible not to.

"Oh, very," she said, unable to stop talking to the girl with a condescending air. She lowered her voice as she fixed her gaze on Evan. Evan, who in addition to getting newly inked, had lost weight, gotten a tan, and was sporting a new, spiky hairstyle that did nothing to hide his receding hairline. He was trying too hard to fit in with his new company, definitely, but even though he looked silly, *Diana* felt like the silly one. "I didn't expect to see you here."

He laughed and wrapped an arm around his young bride-to-be, beaming down at her. "Well . . . funniest thing. I was telling Tilly here all about the trip you had planned, and she said she's never been to Europe and always wanted to go, ever since she was a little girl."

So, like, five years ago. Something about it sounded fishy. "Is that right? Because I know you were just in Haiti a few—"

"Yes! I know. But I checked with work, had to do a little organizing so I could find a couple of free days I could take, and here we are."

Diana just stared, trying to keep her heart rate from rising. How many times when they were married had she begged him to take her to

Europe? How many times had he said "maybe next year" because he simply couldn't get away from his all-important job? They barely went anywhere during their marriage. She'd planted brochures around the house, told him every birthday it was at the top of her list, and every time she watched a movie set in Europe, she'd sigh and tell him it was her dream. And he'd always found a way to get out of it.

But it turned out, it really didn't take very much to convince him.

Just an empty head with two massive balloons and a lot of hair attached to it, who was now nibbling on his ear.

"Oh. How nice." Her voice was wooden. She couldn't help it.

Not that Evan noticed. At this point, the poor fool was so taken by the Vidal delusion that he wouldn't notice if a cruise ship swam upriver and knocked them all into the Arno. Vidal whispered something in his ear, and his goofy grin widened. He dropped his hand behind her, around her slim waist. "So where are you staying, love?"

Diana pressed her lips together, not sure if she could take any more. Knowing Evan, he'd suggest getting together for lunch, which would be the equivalent, fun-wise, of eating lunch with a bunch of angry hornets. This was where Diana would grab her phone, check the display, and rush off, saying she was too busy to talk.

Only when she pulled it out did she remember that it didn't really have much of display. She flipped it open but in the sun glare, couldn't see the screen. She cupped a hand around it and checked the time. "Uh . . . I've got to—"

"Oh my gosh! Is that an actual flip phone?" Tilda exclaimed, erupting with that horrible laugh again. "I haven't seen one of those in years."

"Yes, I lost my phone and all the iPhones are on back—"

"My mom had one when I was a baby! She used to let me play with it."

"Yes, it's almost an antique, hmm," Diana said, unamused. "I do have to go. I just got here today and I have to—"

"Aw, so soon?" Evan said, his brow crinkling. "Are you sure? I mean, it's so great that we just ran into you like this. What are the chances, huh?"

Really, the chances were not great, come to think of it. Sometimes she could walk circles around the supermarket in NYC, a place of fewer than five hundred square feet, and never find a single bottle of ketchup. The fact that in this whole wide world, she and her ex were together, in this spot, now? It was almost too great to be a coincidence.

Maybe it wasn't.

After all, she'd told the kids where she was off to next. Maybe Vidal simply had to show up here, with him, to flaunt their relationship in her face. Maybe this was all a young woman's insane jealousy, rearing its ugly head. Not that she had anything to be jealous of. In the fight for Evan's heart, the young strumpet had won. Hands-down.

Did Vidal actually have something in her head besides air? Diana had to wonder.

"Yes. It's crazy. And really nice running into both of you. Best of luck on the upcoming nuptials. But I do have to go. I have an . . . engagement that I'm late for," she lied, taking a step back and ramming into a man wheeling a cart of gelato down the street. She jumped forward, embarrassed. Ow. That would probably leave a bruise on her backside.

Evan continued, undaunted. He reached a hand out for her, which she quickly snatched away before he could make contact. "But later tonight? We were going out for a celebratory dinner at one of the best restaurants in town. Why don't you come along?"

Diana's eyes widened with visions of angry hornets attacking her from all sides. "Uh, no. Really, I just got into town and . . ."

"Oh, come on, Di. I insist! We should all be together."

We should? What is this, some warped version of Three's Company? Diana's eyes shifted to Vidal. Vidal's nostrils flared in a bit of a sneer, as if she wanted Evan to shut up almost as much as Diana did. She wrapped her claw-like arms around his arm, clutching it possessively, blinking her false eyelashes rapidly. "Honey, she said n—"

"Oh. I forgot to tell you. Lily and Bea will be there. So when I said all of us, I meant, *all* of us. One big, happy family. Me and all my girls!"

"I'm sorry. What did you just say?" Diana couldn't hide her shock. He had to be pulling her leg. She was closer to her daughters than he was. Naturally, since they had that mother-daughter bond. She'd been in touch with them only a couple days ago, and nowhere, no how, had it been mentioned that either of them would be flying out to Italy.

He nodded. "It's true."

Okay, yes, maybe it had been a bit longer than a few days. She'd gotten a few messages from them, but hadn't actually spoken to either of them, because she'd been so busy shuttling from one place to the next. Now, with her phone missing, she'd never know what those messages said.

Still, the more she mulled this new information, the surer she became that her ex was off his rocker. Lily was pregnant, and could never get away from her real estate business, and Bea had a busy schedule, teaching ESL in Japan. No way could they drop everything to be on their way to Florence right now for some celebratory dinner for a marriage they both thought was absolutely ridiculous. She was sure of it. "It can't be. I don't believe you."

He laughed, obviously pleased with himself for giving her this shock of her life. Funny, when they were married, he'd been so level. So predictable. He wasn't one to jet off to Florence or give her any surprises, ever. "What do you need me to do, produce them? They're coming on a flight later this afternoon. I convinced them, last-minute. Paid their way and everything. I know how much they work and wanted to give them some time off, to be with family . . ."

She fisted her phone in her hand. Had she known their numbers, she could . . .

"You could call them," Evan said, grinning. "If that thing works for actual phone calls?"

The more she stood there, waiting for him to tell her he was joking, the less likely it became. He had no motive for joking. Actually, Even didn't have much of a sense of humor at all.

So that meant only one thing . . .

He was telling the truth.

Her stomach sank. Not because she wouldn't have loved to see her kids again. She wanted to, of course. Yes, this trip was for her, so she could find herself, but she did miss them. But having to navigate a dinner with Vidal in order to do it? It hurt. Like a dagger, right to her chest.

So she did what she'd always done, all twenty-eight years of their marriage. She took a deep breath, straightened her spine, smiled, and sucked it up.

She checked the display on her phone. It was getting late. If she wanted to do dinner with them, she'd probably have to get back to the hotel right away. "All right. What time?"

CHAPTER FIVE

Diana stood in the gorgeous, antique fruitwood full-length mirror, surrounded by her beautifully romantic hotel room, and smoothed her simple travel frock down over her hips. She cocked her hip and attempted her sexiest, most come-hither pose.

Her shoulders slumped. *I look like a total frump.*

Surroundings like these demanded a romantic, flowing dress, with lots of lace and layers. They demanded something other than what Diana had packed into her small carry-on suitcase. The dressiest thing she'd brought with her was this—a simple black wrinkle-free dress with no frills. She'd told herself that if she needed anything fancier, she'd go shopping for it, but after leaving Evan and Vidal giggling over the diamond necklace he was buying her to match the rock on her finger, she hadn't been in the mood.

She fixed a couple of simple gold hoops to her ears, fluffed her hair, and applied some deep red lipstick. Not that it helped, but at the moment, she didn't really care.

The main object of the game tonight: *Get through it as quickly as possible.*

At least she'd have Lily and Bea there. But still, as she grabbed her purse and headed downstairs, every fiber of her being wanted to drag her back up to her room and bury herself under the comforter.

There was only one way to get through this: alcohol.

Diana headed to the downstairs bar, overlooking the vineyard, and ordered a Chianti. It was empty there, so she took her glass to the outdoor patio, to enjoy the warm weather. At least one good thing could come out of this nightmare night. After tonight, she'd distance herself from the happy couple and resume her vacation, on her own terms. Who knew? Maybe Bea or Lily would want to go shopping or see the sights with her while they were in town. That would be nice.

As she drained her glass and looked over the vineyards, the dark grapes sagging on their vines, heavy with juice, a calm settled over her. She'd get through it, just like she got through everything in life—with dignity and grace. *Don't worry about it. Tomorrow, you can have fun.*

21

"Methinks the lady doth protest too much," a man suddenly said behind her.

For a moment, Diana thought the words were directed at her, but then she realized a young couple was sitting there, not far from her. The woman, her hair in braids, making her look younger than her years, was probably about Bea's age. She pouted. "I'm serious, Dan. I don't want to go to Verona. It looks awful. I thought you were going to take me to the beach. That's what you promised."

"I will, but I also thought . . ."

"No! I don't want to go to some stupid Shakespeare Festival in the mountains. You're ruining everything. And on my first trip to Italy."

Diana snorted. She hoped she hadn't raised her girls to be such brats. The poor man was obviously just trying to please his girlfriend. And Verona? Who wouldn't want to see Verona? The home of *Romeo and Juliet*? It was another place on Diana's bucket list. It must be terribly romantic.

The man's voice was pleading. "We can go, darling. Later. But the festival's going to start tomorrow. But don't you want to see the city of Verona?"

She crossed her arms tightly over her chest. "No, not unless it has a beach!" she snarled, the chair scraping on the stones as she pushed away from the table and stormed off.

Diana ventured a glance at the man. He looked at her, smiled, and shrugged, like *What can you do?*

I would've gone with you, Diana thought, as the man walked away.

Diana slid off her chair and noticed a brochure spread out on the table that the couple had just abandoned. She went over to it and lifted it up. Sure enough, it was for a summer-long Shakespeare festival in Verona, with music, special events, shopping, and, of course, theater. Diana studied the photograph of the crowded outdoor theater-in-the-round, with people dressed in Elizabethan doublets and ruffs acting on stage. She imagined herself there, and shivered from the thrill of it all.

This was what she wanted to do.

Not some horrible dinner where she had to pretend to be happy for her ex-husband while he fawned over some brainless tart.

But she couldn't back out now. Grabbing her purse, she went through to the lobby and stopped at the concierge. *"Ciao,"* she said to the man at the desk. "Can you call me a cab?"

"Yes, *signora*. Where to?"

She opened her purse and pulled out the slip of paper that Evan had given her. "*Ora d'Aria?*"

As he picked up the phone to call, she noticed the same brochure for the Shakespeare festival that she'd seen outside. "How far away is Verona, from here?" she asked him once he'd finished making the call.

"It is about a three-hour train ride," he said, as she pulled open the brochure and gazed at the photographs of the old city.

"How do I reserve tickets?"

"You may do that here, *signora*," he said, typing away on the computer in front of him. "Two tickets for tomorrow at nine a.m. would be eight hundred forty euros."

"Two? Oh." She shook her head. "No. It would just be me."

"*Oh, scusatemi, signora.* Then four-twenty euros, for just you." Maybe it was just her imagination, but he seemed to look her over with a glance that said, *And what is wrong with you?* His eyes landed on her frumpy dress, pausing there, as if he'd found the reason.

She crossed her arms over her chest, thanked the man, and headed out to wait for the cab. She'd get her ticket to Verona later. Right now, she had dinner with the family to think about.

*

"Mommy!" a voice called from the bar of the restaurant, the second Diana stepped inside.

Suddenly, a tall, dark-haired, blue-eyed and gorgeous woman flung herself into Diana's arms. Though her youngest looked different, she hugged very much the same, as if trying to squeeze the life out of her. Diana smiled. "Oh, it's so good to see you."

It'd been too long, over thirteen months, since Bea had left the United States to teach in Japan. Bea was Diana's wanderer child, her free spirit. She never stayed in place for too long. "Same here, Mommy," she said, pulling away so that they could look at each other.

Diana probably had a few more wrinkles, since the divorce hadn't exactly been kind to her, but Bea had blossomed. Gone was the college-aged girl in the messy bun, glasses, and shapeless sorority sweatshirt. Now, she had a sleek, short pixie-cut and a feminine pink sundress which enhanced her small frame. The same freckles were scattered across the bridge of her nose, though. "You look lovely. Where is Hai?"

23

Bea laughed. "Bring him? Please. This is a girls' trip!" She laughed. "Well, except for Dad."

Just then, Lily appeared between them and hugged her. Lily was even taller than Bea, with the long, more serious face of her father. She was a classic beauty, statuesque and trim, with long raven hair like Diana's, and the bright blue eyes of Evan. "Yeah, Mick was happy to get rid of me." She snickered. "Just kidding. He had to work. As usual. You know him, nose to the grindstone all the time."

As she pulled away, Diana couldn't resist peeking at her tummy. Still flat . . . but was that perhaps the hint of a bulge there? "Well, I'm glad to see you both."

"Mom. I can't believe you agreed to this," Lily muttered. "If this isn't the most dysfunctional family dinner . . ."

Diana had to agree on that one. "I couldn't not! When he told me you two were going to be here . . . what was I supposed to do?"

Bea's jaw dropped and she exchanged a glance with her sister. "Wait . . . Dad told us that you were coming, and that's why he said he wanted us here. Are you telling us that you had no idea about this?"

Diana shook her head. "No, what do you mean? I only found out about it this afternoon, when I saw him at Ponte Vecchio. I was surprised to find him there."

Lily, the skeptic, squinted. "Something smells fishy to me."

"Definitely. Something's up. Well, come on," Bea said, grabbing Diana's hand and smirking at her as she led her through the crowded restaurant. "Let's not keep the happy couple waiting. Just a warning. Vidal's already had two glasses of wine, so she's a little *happy*."

They'd gotten a tight corner booth with a bench seat that went all the way around a circular table. Vidal was on the very end, and thankfully, Bea knew to slide all the way in to sit next to her dad. Lily went next, and Diana sat on the other end, right across from Vidal.

It was an unfortunate position, to say the least. Tilda was wearing a red dress that had perhaps less material than the one she'd been wearing earlier that day, if that was even possible. From Diana's spot, she could see straight down the plunging V of the form-fitting gown, almost to her navel. Her abundant hair was down and so full that it needed its own place at the table, and her face was so made-up, she looked like one of those Bratz dolls her kids used to play with.

As Diana got comfortable, Evan poured her a glass of wine from one of two bottles on the table. At least he hadn't forgotten her choice of white over red. Tilda giggled and kicked her under the table with a sharp kitten heel. Probably an accident, but pain shot up her leg. Tilda leaned forward and took another sip of her wine, her eyes bleary. "Nice dress, Mrs. . . . um, Diana. Is it okay if I call you Diana?"

Diana smiled. At that moment, she preferred it. "I love your dress, too."

Tilda looked down and jutted her boobs out in a way that made every male in the place take notice. "Thanks. Evan bought it for me. He's so sweet."

Evan grinned. Until that moment, Diana had thought he had taste. She hadn't realized he was into the painted-on, Frederick's of Hollywood look.

Bea looked over at her father. "Mom says she didn't know about this little soiree until this afternoon. So how did it come about?"

Evan's goofy grin disappeared. "What do you mean? It was perfectly innocent. I call it serendipity."

Tilda nodded and lifted her glass. "Yes! To serentiddity!"

Bea burst out laughing. Lily elbowed her.

Diana laughed. She could definitely drink to that. And she did.

Evan beamed around the table at them, just as the waiters arrived with plates of food. "Diana. I hope you don't mind. I took the liberty of ordering for us all. It's all family-style here, and everything's incredible, from what I hear."

Diana shook her head. The faster they ate, the faster she could leave this circus. "How kind of you."

The plates were set down. Big, heaping piles of some seafood dish with mussels, a dish of cavatelli in a blush vodka sauce, bruschetta, and a vegetable dish made of mushrooms. It all smelled wonderful, though Diana didn't have much of an appetite.

Lily took a sip of her Perrier, then reached over and grabbed a slice of bread from the basket, dredging it in oil. "Mom, I've called you three times in the past three days and you never got back to me. What have you been doing? I thought an axe murderer—"

"Oh, don't be silly." Lily was her worrier.

Bea nodded in agreement. "We were taking bets on how long it would be before you decided to come home. Dad already lost. He said you'd be back in the first week."

Diana's mouth opened. "Really?" She glanced at her companions around the table, speechless. So, what? They'd been sitting around, discussing her craziness, without her? Sure, she'd done something rash, but at least she hadn't gone and proposed to someone half her age. She'd discussed Evan's mid-life crisis with her kids, but she hadn't even thought about taking bets to see how long the marriage would last.

Evan shrugged, clearly embarrassed. "Well, Di. We all know how much you like to have control. And a trip like this requires a fair amount of flex—"

"I don't like to have control that much!" she said, laughing.

They all stared back at her, as if to say, *Blind much?*

"Forget it." She set her glass down and pulled out a pen, and slid a napkin toward her. "I lost your numbers when I lost my phone."

Bea's mouth was full of pasta. She swallowed and gasped as if Diana had lost a major body part. "You lost your phone?"

Diana nodded.

"Oh my god!" Now, Lily was joining in on the shock.

"Girls. It's not a big deal. I have to wait for the iPhone, but in the meantime, I have this thing." Diana pulled out the old dinosaur and set it down on the table for their inspection. "Like I said. I'm not as big a control freak as you might think! Can I have your numbers? It takes me forever to add in contacts on it, so I'll do it tonight."

Bea lifted it and opened it. "Oh my god. What—Why—" Her mouth made all sorts of beginnings to questions before settling on one. "What, did you not think you could afford a new phone? This thing is practically useless."

Diana's eyes rose to the ornate chandelier above. "I did. Of course I could afford a new phone. But it's on backorder. Besides, it might be a good thing to try to ween myself off my phone. I recommend you try it. There's a whole other world out there, girls, and it's lovely."

Bea looked at her as if she'd just suggested stapling her own eyelids open instead of imbibing her morning coffee. She reached over and petted her iPhone, resting on the table next to her. "No, thanks. I like my phone."

Tilda unleashed that laugh, so loud that it was almost as effective as her boobs in making everyone in the vicinity turn to look at them. "Can you believe it, BB?" she said, looking over at Bea. "I said we haven't seen one of those things since we were like, in diapers!"

Bea scowled at her. She never did like being called BB. Then she pulled out her phone. "Mom, do you know your number? I'll just call you and you can add it."

She gave it to her, and a moment later, her phone rang. She added all of their numbers. Evan slid his over to her. "Just add mine."

Diana picked it up and noticed a lock screen picture of Tilda against a crystal ocean and pink sunset in Haiti, holding a tropical drink and wearing an almost-obscene pink bikini. It was almost like he was rubbing it in her face. She quickly shoved the cell back over to him. "Just get my number from the kids, if you want it."

He shrugged and put it away.

"Oh. Girls. Don't text me. I don't think my phone allows texts. Or if it does, I don't think they can be very long."

Suddenly, Tilda guffawed as she twirled her long hair around a finger. "Oh my *gawd*! That thing doesn't even text? What's it for, then?"

"It's for people who have other priorities in life than their phones," she replied tersely.

Tilda snorted and once again kicked her shin under the table. This time, Diana wasn't so sure it was an accident. Now, her shin was practically bleeding, along with her ears, from Vidal's painful laugh. As nice as it was to see the girls, she couldn't take this anymore.

Diana finished her food and slipped her napkin off her lap. "You know, lovelies, I've had a great time, but—"

"Mommy, you're not going!" Bea whined, sounding every bit four years old. "What about dessert? They have tiramisu!"

Diana shook her head. "I'm sorry. I really do have to go. I have an early morning tomorrow," she lied. "Very busy."

"Oh?" Evan wiped his mouth with his napkin. "Where are you headed?"

There was no way she was going to spill that information. She wasn't sure what had happened here in Florence, but she wasn't going to chance it happening again. "Just doing a little sightseeing." She looked at the girls. "I'll call you two later."

Evan looked a bit shell-shocked. "What . . ." He motioned to Tilda to get up so that he could slide himself out. When she did, rather annoyed by the direction, he rose to his full height and leaned in to kiss her cheek. "I wish you wouldn't leave so soon. We were having a nice night. And who knows . . . if you're going to be in Europe for as long as you say, I might not see you again for a long, long time."

Good, she thought, smiling up at him. "If you do, consider that *serentiddity.*"

27

Then she turned to walk out of the crowded restaurant. She had some serendipity of her own to arrange—and it involved a one-way ticket to Verona and the Shakespeare festival.

CHAPTER SIX

It was a beautiful night, warm and temperate, and the hotel wasn't far away. Since Diana was wearing her sensible shoes—all she'd brought with her—she decided to walk it. As she traveled down the winding street, admiring the symmetry of the Elizabethan architecture in various edifices, she came upon a piazza with bowl-shaped lights and a fountain with a Roman goddess. The gardens sprang to life in the fading Tuscan sunlight, buzzing with fireflies and other insects. Across the street, from a corner café, romantic accordion music wafted through the air.

On the narrow walk, she navigated around couples, strolling arm-in-arm, and sighed.

Florence was nice, but yes. It would be nicer still to be in love here. To share this with someone who she cared about, who cared about her.

Night fell and the stars popped out as she meandered home, still thinking.

There was no doubt about it. Her family obviously still thought she was insane. She'd dropped everything—family, job, house, obligations—to come out here for a year. And though she often thought that she might've made a mistake, a big part of her believed that she was on a great quest, one that was not nearly complete.

So yes, maybe she was crazy. Maybe this was a mid-life crisis.

But it was *her* mid-life crisis. *Her* mistake to make. *Her* life, and for the first time, she was calling the shots, living it the way *she* wanted.

If they didn't like it, they could go shove it.

And maybe that was better than being in love—that she could write this story the way she wanted to, without input from anyone else.

Still . . .

No. She refused to think about it. This was her show. She called the shots. And right now, she was going to make this trip everything she wanted it to be. Because she was in control.

As the castle's lights came into view, she suddenly noticed how dark it was around her. Clouds had rolled in, blocking out the stars.

29

Suddenly, lightning slit the sky, and it began to rain. No, it bordered a torrential downpour.

She broke into a run, laughing when she realized she was already drenched. It didn't make much of a difference what she did.

Of course. *Sure, I'm the one in control.*

*

She took a warm shower under the waterfall shower head in the expansive stall shower, trying to warm up after that drenching rain had nearly chilled her to the bone. Afterwards, she wrapped her body in one of the fluffy hotel robes and sat on the canopy bed, staring at the brochure for the Verona Shakespeare Festival until it was etched in her head.

As beautiful as Florence was, it did feel like the place had been tainted. How many times had she dreamed of Ponte Vecchio? And now, every time she pictured it, she thought of Vidal, bouncing around and laughing that annoying laugh of hers.

The more she thought about it, the surer she became. She needed to get away.

Somewhere new.

Somewhere else on her bucket list.

It was after nine now. The girls had probably ended the dinner with their father. When she picked up her phone and entered in their numbers, she had her mind made up.

She called Bea's phone first, since that was the first number she found while scrolling her confusing contacts list.

"Hello?"

"Hi, darling. It's Mom."

"Mommy. You scooted out so fast, we didn't even have a chance to say goodbye to you."

"I know. I'm sorry."

"I can't really blame you. Vidal's ridiculous. You know she got so drunk, she fell flat on her face when we were leaving?"

"Really?" For some reason, that made Diana feel better. "Was she okay?"

"Oh, sure. Every man in the vicinity rushed to help her. She loved the attention."

Diana sighed. "Well, the wine was very good there." *Though not much else.* "Oh. And I loved seeing you."

"Speaking of which, Mom. Are we going to see you again? We don't fly back for another three days."

"That depends. I'm going to Verona tomorrow. Why don't you two come with me? I'd love to spend more time with you."

"Verona? Where's that?"

"It's about three hours north by train. It's where *Romeo and Juliet* was set. They have a summer-long Shakespeare festival, and—"

"But wait. Didn't you just get here? Why—" She paused, and Diana could hear her talking to someone in the background. "Exactly. Why would you go all the way—"

"Who are you talking to?"

"Lily. We're rooming together. Like old times." She paused. "But seriously, Mom. Lily and I thought we all could go sightseeing around here. We wanted to—"

"I know, love. But I just have a feeling that I need to . . . escape . . ."

"This is because of Dad, isn't it?"

"No," she said immediately, a lie that must've been pretty transparent, considering how quickly Bea returned with, "Oh, yes it is."

"Well—"

"Like I said. I don't blame you. You were trying to escape him and Vidal, and he shows up on your—"

"I was not trying to escape them." Well, she had been, a little. Them, and about a thousand other things about her mundane, ordinary life. But yes, them showing up had thrown a complete wrench into her purpose, which was writing her own post-marriage chapter, sans Evan. "And I'm definitely not trying to escape you. If you want to come along, I'll be taking the nine o'clock tomorrow morning. You can come with me."

"Hold on. Let me ask Lil." She didn't sound that enthusiastic. There was a pause. When she came back on, she said, "We'll come. But we'll probably take a later train out. Lil wants to see the Cathedral."

"Okay. That's fine. I'll meet you there. It'll be fun." As she said it, a thought occurred to her. Florence was supposed to be fun, too. It *would've* been, if Evan and Vidal hadn't shown up and changed the entire romantic fabric of the city for her. She quickly added, "But Bea . . ." wondering how to phrase it as delicately as possible. Even though

31

her children were grown, she'd never wanted it to seem like there was animosity between her and Evan. It wasn't healthy to see parents fighting over petty things, no matter how old their kids were.

"I get it, I get it. Don't tell Dad. We won't."

She smiled. "Thank you. So I'll see you tomorrow? Tex—" She stopped, remembering her phone. "Call me when you get in, all right?"

"I will. Good night, Mom. Love you."

Diana ended the call and flipped her phone closed. Verona. Tomorrow. Sure, *Romeo and Juliet* had been a tragedy, but Diana was determined to make her own experience in Italy a happy one, no matter what it took.

CHAPTER SEVEN

At promptly 8:45 the following morning, Diana boarded the Italia-Rail train to Verona. As she settled into her seat in the crowded train, she smiled, feeling almost like she had in New York when she'd left Evan behind the first time—a mix of excitement and nerves.

Of course, though the train was practically full, no one sat next to her. Some people even seemed to want to stand, rather than sit beside or across from her at her table. She kept the seat clear, and yet, people took one look at her and went elsewhere. After a while, she started to get a complex. Did she smell? Look evil? What?

She picked up her menu and read the offerings, trying not to worry too much about it.

Before the train left, a waiter came by and asked her if she wanted something to drink. "A Perrier, I guess," she said, since her stomach was a bit unsettled from all the wine last night.

"And your husband?" He motioned to the seat across from her.

Oh, so that was it. "Oh, no. I'm alone."

He raised his eyebrows, confused, as if she'd just admitted she was a cannibal.

Diana almost laughed. She was no longer wearing her wedding band, and hadn't worn it in over a year, so the line from it on her finger had faded. What was it about her that made her look like she was still a part of a couple? Was it her age, her demeanor, her conservative dress and hairstyle? Did she have to dress or carry herself a certain way in order to look single? How did one meet eligible single men her age, then?

Maybe it was just that she looked too eligible. Too desperate to meet men.

Yes, that was probably it. Wasn't there an old adage about men usually flocking to a woman, the second she stopped looking for one?

That thought nestled firmly in her mind, she turned toward the window and watched as the train station was left behind. Only a mile or so later, the buildings of Florence gave way to rolling countryside and vineyards. Cows and livestock roamed stone-fenced meadows, and ramshackle barns and farmhouses studded the verdant green fields. In the distance, the magnificent Dolomites rose up, their snow-capped ridges scraping the bright blue sky.

"*Scusi*," a voice said suddenly, stirring her from her awe.

She looked up, expecting it was the waiter, ready to take her order. But it was a tall, slim, dark-haired man in a suit jacket, with a leather bag over his shoulder. "Oh, I'm sorry. Yes?"

"American?" He smiled, and the corners of his eyes crinkled in amusement. He pointed to the seat across from her. "Is that seat taken?"

"No. Not at all."

She shifted her drink and book closer to her, to make room for him, but he held up a hand as he slipped off his jacket. "Not necessary, thank you," he said politely in a clipped Italian accent, then slipped in the seat and let out a tired sigh.

"You've been traveling a lot," she observed.

He looked down at himself and laughed. "Is it that obvious?"

She shook her head, immediately embarrassed for making him feel self-conscious. He was very clean, really, considering. She'd looked and felt far worse after her jaunt across the Atlantic. But he had more than a five o'clock shadow, studded with gray hair, and his eyes were a bit bleary. "Not at all. You just look tired."

He laughed. "I should be. I've been flying since yesterday morning. Just got in from New York."

"Oh? I'm from New York myself. You're from Italy?"

"Yes," he said, motioning to the waiter and ordering an espresso. "Verona is my home. Very happy to be returning. I am Marcello."

He reached out a hand. She took it. "Diana."

He shook it lightly, slowly, and with meaning, dipping his head with reverence, and for a moment, she thought he might kiss her knuckles. "Lovely to meet you, Princess Diana."

The gesture was so unexpected, a giggle erupted from Diana's throat. "Um. Just Diana is fine."

"But you look like a princess. Like you should have an entourage of admirers."

Diana blinked. She'd heard Italian men were forward with women, taking what they wanted. So . . . did that mean that Marcello wanted her? She started to flush and looked away.

"It is my first visit," Diana said. "And it's fortunate you sat down here because I was wondering what I should see. I'm only in town for the day, I'm thinking. I'll be taking a late train back to Florence. Of course, if you'd rather rest . . ."

"No, no." He laughed. "I am happy to tell you. Verona is the most beautiful town, full of tradition and history. You will like. You go to Castle Vecchio, of course."

Diana wasn't sure she wanted to go to *anything* Vecchio, at all, since Ponte hadn't worked out so well for her. But *Vecchio* was Italian for "old," so she assumed that if she wanted to absorb the country's history, she needed to break with that fear as soon as possible. "Is it nice?"

The waiter came with his espresso, and he lifted the tiny cup. "Very. You like. Very nice *ponte*, there, too. Lovely views of the river."

"*Ponte?*" Her stomach roiled as her head swam with flashbacks of the last *Ponte.*

"Bridge. *Si.*"

Hmm. The last thing she wanted was to think about her interaction with Evan and Vidal. "Any other ideas?"

"Let's see. You can go to the *Piazza delle Erbe* to do some shopping, eh? Or . . . Piazza Bra, which is beautiful and historic. Oh. And you must come to the Shakespeare Festival. It is so good. Music, wine, food, dancing. Period costumes. Very famous."

She smiled, though she wasn't sure she wanted to see a period costume again in her lifetime. She'd done that in Versailles, and the adventure had turned out far from the romantic time she'd been expecting. "That sounds nice. I'd heard about it. I was definitely thinking of stopping by."

"You should," he said, gesturing wildly with his hands. "It is something you will always remember!"

She laughed at his enthusiasm and obvious love for his hometown. But Versailles had turned out to be something she'd always remember, too, and not for all good reasons, either. In fact, it'd been a bit scary for a time, considering she'd wound up a suspect in a murder and jewel theft. "What were you doing in New York?"

"Oh." He laughed. "Not for much good, I am afraid. I had an audition for a play. Broadway."

"You're an actor?"

He nodded. "Yes. The timing, though, was no good. I did badly. But it was for the part of a lifetime, so I had to take it." He seemed to drift off for a moment, likely remembering something he'd done in the audition, and shook his head in a self-deprecating way. "It was a disaster."

"Oh. I'm sure it wasn't that bad," she said. The man was handsome, an Italian Pierce Brosnan. Of course he was an actor. Something told Diana that he'd immediately captivate any audience, in any room he walked into. Yes, he'd likely done just fine in that audition.

"Ah. You weren't there. I forgot my lines. I—" He laughed. "I was exhausted. It's my fault for flying in that morning after dress rehearsal the night before."

"Dress rehearsal?"

"Yes. It was terribly inconvenient that my agent scheduled it that way, considering it was on the eve of . . ." He stopped, as if remembering something. "Diana."

She blinked. He was staring at her as if he had something very important to tell her. Odd, considering they'd just met. "Yes?"

He reached into the pocket of his bag and pulled out a ticket. "You like Shakespeare?"

She nodded. "Very much."

"Then you must be my guest. I am performing in *A Midsummer Night's Dream* at the Arena di Verona this afternoon. It is our famous open-air theater, and I tell you, it is thrilling just to be there inside it. Even better than the Colosseum in Roma! It is opening night. Do me the honor of being my guest?"

She looked at the ticket. It was front seat, center. The idea was exactly up her alley. She'd always wanted to go to Broadway plays, but Evan had never liked them. Though Broadway was only a short drive away, she could count on one hand the number of times she'd been in to watch a performance. The last was *Cats*, in the 1980s, and that had been, well . . . weird.

But she'd always loved *A Midsummer Night's Dream*, from the moment she'd read it in high school. In fact, of all of Shakespeare's plays, it'd been her favorite, since it was so magical and mysterious. She'd always wanted to see it performed. In Italy, at the famous Arena di Verona? That would be a big plus. "Who do you play?"

He smiled. "I'm a mechanical. Peter Quince, the carpenter. It's quite a good production."

"Oh." That was a good role. He had to be very experienced. Well, she supposed him jetting off to New York to audition said that he was a

36

serious actor. And clearly, he was different from Evan, who never understood the arts. That was a *definite* plus. She took the ticket. "You know, *A Midsummer Night's Dream* takes place in Athens. Not Verona. That's *Romeo and Juliet*."

He laughed. "And *Two Gentleman of Verona*, but of course that one is less known. You know your Shakespeare."

Marcello clearly did, too. Maybe that went with the territory of being an actor. She'd never actually met an actor before. Evan likely didn't even know that *Romeo and Juliet* was set in Verona . . . and probably didn't even care. He'd hated Shakespeare. She stared at the ticket, feeling her heart skip with excitement. "I'd love to. Tonight?"

"Today. At three in the afternoon sharp. You'll be there?"

"Yes. Of course. I am sure I will enjoy it." She thought about asking for more tickets, for Lily and Bea, but she didn't want to be pushy. Besides, she didn't know what time they'd arrive. And if the girls wanted to take in a play, which she wasn't really sure they'd even enjoy, since they were more like their father in that respect, she could always buy them tickets later. "Thank you so much."

"You're welcome." He leaned forward and his eyes drifted from her to the window, dancing a little. "Ah. See that little hill?"

She followed his gaze out the window to a small, rising slope, where several sheep were lazily grazing under the bright sun and a sky dotted with cotton clouds. "Yes."

"Beyond that, in that valley, is my home. It is good to be back there. And I know you will love it. Maybe you stay? Perhaps tomorrow, after the performance, I might have the pleasure of meeting you again?"

The thought had never occurred to her. To stay? Luckily she'd brought her large carry-on bag with her rather than leaving her things in Florence, so yes, she supposed she could change plans and stay in Verona overnight, if the situation called for it. But . . . would her obsessively ordered planner's mind let her do that, simply on a whim?

As she stared into Marcello's dark eyes, she didn't care.

She nodded, her breath taken away as she thought of the bucket list item she'd written on the train. *Fall in love in Italy.*

Beyond that hill, a charming city came into view. Maybe there, that dream would come true.

CHAPTER EIGHT

Diana walked down the cobbled streets of Piazza delle Erbe, gazing in the windows of the shops. As she did, the words kept running through her head: *Fall in love in Italy. Fall in love in Italy. Fall in love in Italy.*

Marcello was nice. Handsome. Charming. When he'd left her in front of the train station, where he'd helped her hail a cab to the Piazza, he'd winked at her and told her that he would be looking for her in the audience.

She shivered at the memory, then reminded herself to chill out, as Bea would've said. The last time she'd gotten all googly-eyed over a man had been in Versailles, when she'd danced with a man who turned out to be not only married, but a jewel thief. He'd also been murdered later that night, and she'd been a suspect. *You don't exactly have impeccable taste in men,* she scolded herself as she stepped along the concourse.

Marcello was right. It was a lovely place to go shopping. The square was bordered on all sides by historic buildings, some of them cafes with outdoor, umbrellaed seating. The smell of roast garlic hung heavy in the air. There were many old Roman sculptures, as well as a large fountain in the center. People were sitting at its edge, basking in the sun.

Diana wasn't exactly hungry, though. Well, perhaps she was, but it wasn't for food. There was a strange sense of yearning inside her, one she couldn't quite define.

As she walked by the shops, peering in the windows, her phone began to buzz in her pocket. She didn't recognize the number, but she answered anyway. It was Lily. "Mom. Just wanted to let you know we're at the train station in Florence. We've got tickets for the two o'clock."

"Oh, great! I'll see you tonight. I'm going to a show. Would you want me to try to get you tickets?"

"A show?"

"Yes. *A Midsummer Night's Dream.*"

38

"Ew. Why?"

So that was a no. Diana burst out laughing. That was exactly what she thought Lily would say. "Contrary to your belief, some people actually enjoy Shakespeare's plays."

She laughed, too. "Doubtful. With who?"

"What?"

"Who are you going with?"

"No one. I'm going by myself, of course," Diana said, wondering what happened to solo travel. Why was it so shocking to people? "But the town is beautiful. You'll love it."

She sighed. "I loved Florence. I could've spent the next week there. As it is, Mom, we only have three days. And until this little wrench, we were thinking about going to Rome."

"Oh. Sorry about that," she said. "If you'd rather, you can—"

"Mom. Stop making it sound like you're trying to get rid of us!"

"I'm not, love," she said. She wasn't, but she hadn't expected to see her kids. She'd said her goodbyes two weeks ago. To see them so soon was lovely, but it she'd mentally prepared herself for a much longer time away from them. "But this is my trip, and I want to—"

"I don't get it. Who are you and what have you done with Diana St. James?"

"What are you talking about, darling?"

"You're being so . . . weirdly . . . spontaneous. Need I remind you that you were the one who scheduled us down to the minute during that Disney vacation? What happened to that woman? Because picking up and changing locales on the spur of the moment was really—"

"Necessary," she said. "I didn't make the choice lightly. But I'm learning that sometimes it's better to pay attention to one's heart than what's posted on my planner."

"Oh. My. God." There was a pause. Likely, she was discussing this newest revelation with Bea. "I wish you'd have learned that twenty years ago, when I wanted to go on Dumbo twice but you just *had* to get us to our appointments at the Bibbity Bobbity Boutique."

"*You* wanted those makeovers," Diana pointed out.

"Forget it," Lily grumbled. "Anyway. I'll call you when we get to Verona. Enjoy the play. We can go to dinner."

When she pocketed her phone, she knew exactly what the yearning was when she peered into a shop window and saw a sky-blue dress with flutter sleeves.

Yes, that was what she wanted.

She'd been so embarrassed, wearing that black travel dress, which was now in a ball in the bottom of her carry-on. Not only had it made her look like wallpaper, she'd felt that way, too. What she needed was something that would help her stand out. Feel pretty, feminine. Something for tonight.

A bell over the door jingled as she went inside. The place was dark, the walls and floor covered in royal-red carpet and wallpaper, and choked with displays of an array of clothing. It was a secondhand shop, yet all of the mannequins were dressed so beautifully, Diana had a hard time believing anyone would part with the clothes.

A woman came out from behind a glass case. *"Ciao,"* she started, and began speaking in very fast Italian.

"I'm sorry," Diana said. "I don't speak Italian well and I've lost my translator, so could you please speak slowly? *Per favore parla più lentamente?"*

The woman was wearing a leopard-print blouse, and she had all of her dark hair pulled back from her head in a giant barrette with a unicorn on it. She was older, with thick cake makeup gathering in the wrinkles around her eyes and on her lips. "Ah, I speak English," she said. "Can I help you?"

"Yes, thank you. I was interested in that dress in the front window."

The woman's eyes lit up. "Oh, yes. One of my proudest moments!"

"You made it?"

The woman laughed. "Of course. This is my store. I make everything in here. One of a kind!"

"Oh." At that moment, Diana was determined to have that dress. But with the luck she'd had lately, she also felt sure something would stand in her way. "What size is it?"

"Size two."

Well, there it was. That left her out.

"But all of my dresses can be let in and out for a perfect, custom fit," she said with a smile, going over to the window. She pulled the dress form down and began to take the dress off. From this angle, Diana realized that the fabric was blue with tiny stars. "Let's try it on."

"All right," Diana said, letting the woman lead her through racks stuffed with dresses, to a single dressing room in the back of the building with a red velvet curtain.

The woman swept it aside dramatically and ushered her in. "It was calling to you, no? I think dresses do. I could already tell this one belongs to you."

If it did belong to me, it wouldn't be a size two, she thought, quickly undressing as she looked at the dress on the hanger in front of her. *Well. Fingers crossed.*

She took a deep breath and slipped it on. Miraculously, not only did it fit, but it hugged her curves nicely, with plenty of room. It didn't even accentuate her little stomach pooch. And it looked lovely, with the sweetheart neckline and graceful, flowing skirt with several layers. She stood up on her tiptoes, pretending to be in heels, and gathered her hair up, imagining herself sitting in the audience of the old theater.

Yes, it's very nice, she thought to herself as she twirled around a bit. *But I don't have shoes and I don't know how much it costs . . .*

She pulled open the curtain to find the woman standing there with a pair of strappy heels that matched the silver-blue hue of the dress almost exactly. "These look like your size."

Stunned, Diana slipped her feet into them, feeling like Cinderella as they fit her feet exactly, without pinching at all. And the heel wasn't anything that would break her neck, either. At that moment, as she gazed at herself in the mirror and swished the skirt around her knees, she knew that whatever the price, they belonged to her.

It felt like . . . like . . . *serendipity.*

She looked up at the woman, beaming at her reflection in the mirror, and smiled. "I'll take them."

*

Diana would have looked up the Arena di Verona prior to taking a cab to it from the shopping district, but without a phone, that was impossible. It didn't matter. While she was changing in the dressing room, she'd noticed a photograph of it. In fact, it looked very much like the Colosseum, though smaller, but even better preserved.

But even the photograph did not prepare her for the place in person. She gasped as she stepped out on the curb. The giant Roman amphitheater was full of ornate sculpture, columns, and arches of pink and green blocks. Diana simply could not believe that she'd be spending the afternoon enjoying a performance of Shakespeare, in a place where hundreds of years ago, gladiators would perform bloody and chilling spectacles for audiences.

It was a dream come true, but she quickly tempered her expectations as an usher took her ticket and led her down to her seat, right at the front of the theater. *Remember what happened the last time you got excited about an event, in Versailles? Someone ended up dead.*

She almost laughed at the thought. This was a play, not a bunch of gladiators fighting. The chances of death today were pretty slim.

Because of the age of the theater, the seats were rather small and uncomfortable, but she was right there in the center, so close she could touch the stage. The usher handed her a program, and she paged through it, as two large Italian men took the seats on either side of her.

Squeezed in between them, she sucked in a breath and opened the program. As she paged through it, she noticed with a bit of disappointment that it was all in Italian. She turned to a black-and-white photograph of the man she'd met on the train, the one who was playing Quince. He looked even more handsome in the photograph, with his white shirt, open at the throat, and even more of a beard, his thick dark hair tumbling over his forehead. It almost stopped her heart to look at him, remembering the way he'd smiled at her over the table in the train car.

Marcello Camillo. That was his name.

Without her cell phone to help her translate, she did her best, trying to decode the rest of the small biography. Born and bred in Verona. Recently played the Duke of Venice in *Othello* in last summer's Shakespeare Festival and Horatio in *Hamlet* in the one prior. His television credits included a stint on *All My Children*. Received his M.F.A. from the University of Verona. No mention of family or children, though Diana wasn't sure a bio would include something like that. She stared at the picture for far too long, then paged through the other actors' information with waning interest.

The lights dimmed and a loudspeaker crackled. Someone said something in Italian, which Diana assumed was the usual notice prohibiting flash photography and to silence all phones. She closed the program on her lap and got ready to watch as the crowd around her silenced.

Then the play began. The curtain rose on a woodland scene, as she'd expected. Then, to her excitement, the first actors appeared on stage.

It was the palace of Theseus. Two men and a woman appeared on the stage. With excitement, she leaned forward, ready to hear the gorgeous phrases of the master wordsmith himself.

And then . . .

They spoke.

In Italian.

She listened to the lovely words, not understanding a single one of them. Shakespeare was challenging enough as it was, but in another language, it was quite impossible. The actors seemed good . . . she thought. But by the time Lysander, the mortal young lover of Hermia, arrived—at least, she thought it was Lysander—she had no idea what was going on.

The first scene ended, and then she sucked in a breath as Marcello—as Quince—appeared, dressed in a linen blouse, doublet, hose, and craftsman's apron. She knew the play quite well, though she hadn't seen it since her school years. This was the comedic part where Quince, attempting to put on a rousing theatrical production for Duke Theseus of Athens and the Amazon queen, Hippolyta, arranges all the rather untalented craftsmen of the town to act in the play. There was quite a lot of laughter from the audience, especially at Nick Bottom.

Marcello stole the scene, even with Nick Bottom constantly attempting to. Marcello spoke in such fluid Italian she was instantly hypnotized by his words. He was clearly talented, his voice strong and sure. As he spoke, she found herself zeroing in on him, unable to look at anything else happening on stage. She grew warm, and her bare chest flushed as she watched. For a moment, she could've sworn his eyes drifted toward her, and a smile appeared on his face as he said his lines.

If only she knew what he was saying!

Not that it would've done much good. He was simply reciting the lines to the play.

By the time Puck, the woodland sprite, came jaunting about the forest, she'd lost interest again, but she couldn't stop thinking of Marcello. He was clearly the most talented of all the actors. His presence on the stage had dwarfed them all.

She struggled through the rest of the first half, only perking up every time Quince arrived on the stage. When the curtain fell, signaling intermission, she checked her phone. She had a missed call from Bea.

She ran outside and checked her voicemail. Sure enough, they'd arrived about twenty minutes ago. She called back. Just when she thought the phone was going to ring through to voicemail, Bea picked up. "I forgot you can't text. I sent you a text," she said with a sigh. "Where are you?"

"I'm at that play. It's only intermission. I was thinking about staying at a hotel overnight but I haven't really looked into—"

"Don't worry about it. Enjoy the play. Lily and I found a place right next to the train station so we're having a glass of wine. Just call us when you're done and we'll meet up."

"Are you sure?"

"Very! We're on a patio in downtown Verona, sipping Italian wine on a beautiful summer's day! Well, Lily is having a San Pellegrino, but you know. Things could be a lot worse."

For a moment, Diana wondered if she should skip out and join them. It was the safer, more comfortable thing to do. She looked around at all the people, sipping their intermission drinks from the bar and chatting in Italian. It was probably foolish for her to come to this play when she was so lost by the whole thing. And for what? As much as she had convinced herself it was for the culture, for the once-in-a-lifetime experience of seeing a Shakespeare play in a Shakespearean town, part of her had also been hoping that that dashing actor would . . .

Would *what*, exactly? Call her onstage and profess his love for her?

No, maybe not that. But still, the whole *Fall in love in Italy* thing hung heavily in her mind. Maybe wanting it, being too desperate for it, would only make it impossible.

Still, she hadn't gone on this trip to be safe. She'd gone to step out of her comfort zone. And that was what she was going to do.

"All right, darling, I'll see you in a bit," she said as the lights in the lobby dimmed, signaling the show was about to start. "I must go now."

She flipped her phone closed and headed back to the front row, picking up the pace when she realized most of the theater was already back in their seats. As she got there, she noticed the two burly men that had sandwiched her in earlier. One of them had put his program on her seat.

Before she could get annoyed, though, she moved closer and realized that it wasn't a program. It was a slip of white paper, origami-folded into the shape of a flower.

Squinting, she moved nearer and read the single word on the front. It said, *Diana.*

Her heart skipped a beat as she picked it up and looked around to see if anyone was watching her. She lifted the flaps, her hands trembling, and read:

Princess Diana,

You look so beautiful out there. Please meet me backstage after the show. I'll be waiting for you.

Yours,

M.

CHAPTER NINE

He winked.

At the conclusion of the performance, when the actors came out, Marcello dashed on stage with the other actors, did his final bow, looked right at her, and *winked*.

Diana flushed and applauded as hard as she possibly could, her skin buzzing with the excitement of it all.

When the curtain went down and the applause began to die, Diana stepped into the aisle, realizing she couldn't remember a single thing that had even *happened* during the second half of the play. A couple of times, she'd thought maybe she just dreamt the note, but then she'd find it in her clammy palm, its delicate folds and swaying script a reminder of the care its creator had put into it.

Marcello.

And then, he'd winked.

He wanted to meet her. To . . . start something.

Calm yourself, she said as she climbed the steps of the arena, fanning her face. After all, she'd gotten excited in Paris, only to find out the man wooing her was nothing but a cheating scumbag. She needed to temper her expectations. *If all you get out of it is a signed program from a good actor, that will be enough.*

But she couldn't deny her heart wanted more.

Forcing away those thoughts, she went through the lobby and found the corridor leading backstage. There was a guard waiting there, an old man who didn't look threatening at all, despite his official blue uniform. She smiled at him and showed him the letter from Marcello. He looked at it and said, "Marcello, eh?"

She nodded. It only said "M," though. So what did that mean? Did Marcello often woo women to sit in the front row and ask them to visit him backstage? Was he a player? "How did you know?"

He grinned, and in a deep accent, said, "The folds. Marcello loves origami. He is a true artist with it."

That sounded like a lie. Like he was fudging for a friend. "Oh. How nice," she said, not certain if that was just the guard, covering for him. "The flower was very nice."

The man pushed off his stool and hobbled to the side, letting her pass. He winked at her. "Downstairs. End of hall. Right."

Too late to turn back now. Even if he is a player, you're just going to get your program signed. That's all.

"Thank you," she said, gripping her program in her hands and stepping into the narrow hallway. Because the arena itself was centuries old, she felt as though she was venturing into a crypt. Though Diana wasn't exactly tall, the ceiling was so low that she feared her head would scrape it, and the stone walls around her seemed to weep with rivulets of water. The smell was like moldy copper, and the corridor so dark that she had to brace herself against the wall several times so she wouldn't trip on the uneven stone flooring. As she walked, up ahead, she heard the lively sound of conversation.

When she came to the first door, which was open and said *Pietro Colombo, Direttore*, she found an office, where two men were arguing in Italian. One, who she assumed was the director, Pietro, was holding a clipboard and wearing a headset. The taller of the two men was wearing the Oberon costume and looked pretty upset about something. They both stopped speaking and glared at her as she came forward, as if she'd interrupted them.

Then the large man muttered something under his breath and came lumbering toward her. The hall was so narrow that he had to slip sideways to go past her. As he did, he rapid-fired Italian at her and gestured down the hall, to where she'd come from.

"I'm sorry, I don't . . ." Assuming the man was saying she wasn't allowed back there, she pulled out the note from Marcello and held it up. "I was invited back here by one of your actors?"

He took one look at it and rolled his eyes in disgust, then muttered, *"Marcello e le sue donne."* Before Diana could ask what that meant, he waved her off, then slammed the door.

She passed another room, where she saw several of the fairies from the play, enjoying drinks and chatting. They paid her no mind.

At the third one, she noticed the man who played Lysander, standing in front of his mirror, gesturing to Hermia. *Oh, they were very good,* Diana thought as Lysander, slim and built like a rod, took notice of her. Maybe they would sign her program, too?

47

His eyes narrowed, and he turned, walked to the door, and slammed it in Diana's face.

Diana blinked. Apparently not. Apparently these theater types weren't all that friendly. Well, it was her own fault. She probably shouldn't have been peeking in his dressing room like a clod.

Diana passed about a dozen more rooms, each filled with actors or stagehands, before finally coming to the end of the hallway. Marcello's door was closed, but there was a chalkboard there, and written upon it, *M Camillo.*

Diana Camillo. The thought flittered across her mind before she could tell it to behave. *Come on, Diana. What are you, twelve? Marriage is the last thing you're after. You want your program signed. That's all.*

Still . . . a little, or even a lot, of romance would be nice. After all the disappointment her love life had given her, an ember still burned inside her, forever hopeful. *Fall in love in Italy.*

She reached her hand up to knock, and her knuckles had barely made contact with the door when it flew open. A petite blonde in an Elizabethan costume bustled out, dragging her layers of skirt with her. It was Titania. She took one look at Diana, smirked and let out a small, scoffing laugh, then shut the door behind her and moved past, nearly toppling Diana with that massive dress of hers. Diana had to flatten herself all the way against the weeping wall in order to let her through. She stomped away, muttering something to herself in Italian.

Diana watched her disappear into her own dressing room. And then, she was alone in the hallway. Taking a deep breath, she knocked on the door.

"Come in," a voice called from inside.

She twisted the knob and went in. The room was small, like the others, dimly lit, and smelled like roses and incense. She stepped in. The floor was uneven, rising slightly up to where there was a small dressing table. Marcello was sitting at the tufted bench there, his hands on his knees, wearing his costume and smoking a small black cigarette. Through the smoky haze, he smiled at her and stubbed the cigarette out in an ashtray on the table. "You received my note," he said, turning back to her. "Good. I am delighted to see you."

Was he really? Or did he just get done having a lover's quarrel with Titania?

She let out the breath she was holding. It didn't matter. She was just here to talk to him.

"Yes, um . . . I am glad you invited me back here." *Be calm. Casual. Relaxed.* She held up her program, the front of which was now smeared with the sweat from her hands. "I thought perhaps you could sign my program."

He let out a wry chuckle that suggested he knew much more than she was letting on. It put her off, making her feel like Little Red Riding Hood talking to the Big Bad Wolf.

"Is that what you thought?" he said in a lilting, teasing way as she hovered in the doorway. His brow was beaded with sweat, and his linen blouse hung open at the neck, damp with it, the once-white collar a dark beige with his stage makeup. "Come in, come in. I am not going to bite, Princess Diana."

She took a step forward. She was being silly. She was a grown woman. Why was she acting so timid?

Deeper in the room, it opened to a larger space than she'd noticed from the door. There was a large rack in the corner, stuffed with costumes and clothing, and an oriental-patterned changing screen along the far wall. He motioned to a ruby red sofa that was surrounded by little knickknacks, stuffed animals, and flowers, gifts that he must've been given from admirers. She pushed aside a coat and sat as he turned. She realized he was holding a bottle of wine.

"Interested in sharing a drink with me?" he asked, but the corkscrew was in the cork and he was already prying it out. "I just received this as a gift. Good vintage."

A gift from one of his admirers. Just like all the other gifts around here. Probably, all of these are from women. He is an attractive man.

She shook her head, too nervous to drink. The last thing she needed was to be losing her head here.

He had two glasses sitting on his dressing table, almost as if he'd expected her. Or expected *someone.* Likely, that was his usual modus operandi—inviting a woman to accompany him backstage after his performance; as necessary as that after-performance cigarette or glass of wine. He poured himself a glass and shrugged. "All right. You can help yourself if you'd like. I'd love to talk more and find out all about you, Diana. Mind if I change first?"

Her breath caught. "Here?"

He let out a long, deeply amused laugh, then knelt in front of her. "Oh, Diana." He pointed behind the screen. "You are a funny one. I shouldn't imagine doing anything that would make you uncomfortable. I won't be long."

"Oh, of course," she said, feeling stupid. "That's fine. I'll just wait here."

He took a gulp of his wine, smacked his lips together, and let out an exaggerated, dramatic sigh. Likely he did everything that way, considering he was an actor. "I needed that. After that disastrous performance."

"Disastrous? I thought you were very good."

He chuckled. "Well, thank you. I try. Some of them are a bunch of buffoons, though. I've been with them for a while and some of them are the best at what they do. Others—who knows how they got a place in our company? Certainly not by talent. But we muddled through." He disappeared behind the screen with his glass. "Tell me," he called over the screen. "We never discussed it on the train. What brings you to Europe, all by your lonesome?"

"Oh," she tittered, folding her hands on her lap as she looked around the room. Along with many folded origami shapes—birds, boats, airplanes, animals—there were plenty more possible signs that he'd had *women friends* around. Cards with hearts stuck in the frame of the mirror, one which said, *"Ti amo, Marcello!"* A tube of lipstick on the dressing table—or was that just part of his own stage makeup? A lacy cape that could only have been part of a female's costume, or perhaps an article of clothing left by a female visitor. "I've been wanting to do it all my life. I just decided it was time."

"Time?"

She swallowed back the urge to titter again. *Stop acting like a child!* "Yes, you know. I was bored with the daily grind. I worked as a Vice President of Marketing for Addict Cosmetics in New York, commuted in from Long Island, and every day was the same. So one day, one of my co-workers was talking about her trip to Europe, and I guess you could say I caught the bug. I realized I'd done very little of what I wanted to do, all my life, for what I thought I *had* to do. So I quit my job, put everything in storage, and decided to spend a year over here."

"A year?" he said, and coughed. "My goodness. Really? Where have you been so far?"

He sounded impressed. Again, she fought back the urge to giggle under his attentions. There was one sure way to nip that in the bud. She got up and crossed to the vanity, where she poured herself a glass of wine. She'd only have a little, just to take the edge off.

"I've only been out here a few weeks. I started in Paris. Then Florence. And now, here. Verona." She brought the glass to her lips as she turned and stared at a photo collage on the wall. It included snapshots from what must've been Marcello's entire career. Pictures of him with various actors, young and old. And, wait. Was that Sean Connery?

She moved closer, until her shins were flush against the cushion of the velvet sofa, squinting to see.

"Ah. How'd you like Paris?" he asked, tossing his doublet and apron to hang over the screen.

Yes, she was almost certain it was Sean, in his younger days. In the photograph, Marcello looked very young, too. A teenager, with a thick head of dark hair and a white smile that made him look like he was up to no good. He looked a bit like a young Frank Sinatra. "It was an adventure," she said, scanning over to someone who looked very much like Julia Roberts. He was only a young man in that photograph, but he had his arm draped possessively around her, as they walked some red carpet. She nearly choked. *Did he date Julia Roberts?* "I went to Versailles and got a little bit more than I bargained for."

There was a bit of rustling behind the screen, and then he draped his white undershirt over the top of the frame. He coughed again, and his voice was fainter. It sounded like he was losing interest in her. "Eh? How so?"

Now her eyes caught on a picture of him giving a cheek-kiss to a smiling and delighted-looking Idina Menzel. So, Marcello dallied with A-list celebrities. What was she doing here, with him, when he could be with all of these more exciting, glamorous women? She couldn't stop shivering enough to even think of bringing the wine to her lips without spilling it. Instead, she started to pour out the whole sordid story to him. "Oh, you see, I went to Versailles for their annual ball. And I met an individual who turned out to be a jewel thief, and the necklace I was wearing—the Madame Royale, which was worth over a million dollars—went missing. And then the man was mur—"

THUNK.

The sound made Diana whirl so fast that the drink in the glass sloshed onto her hand. All rustling behind the screen stopped, and a strange silence settled over the room, in which she could only hear the beating of her heart. She was about to ask him if he was all right, when her eyes drifted down to the ground.

Lying there, palm upward, was Marcello's hand, and a few inches from it, his spilled wine glass.

"Marcello?" she asked, though she already know she wouldn't receive an answer, even as she crept forward, revealing more of him—a pale forearm, a shoulder, a chest, clothed only in an undershirt.

But it was when she finally went past the screen and saw his face, eyes wide and empty, staring forever at nothing, his mouth open in a silent scream, that she realized something was very, very wrong.

Letting out a squeak of terror, she backed away, up against the wall, wishing she could unsee that ghastly expression on his face. His chest hadn't been moving, so did that mean . . . was he . . .

Oh, god.

But he'd just been talking to her, and he was fine. Perfect. Virile and strong and happy to be done with the play. And now he was . . .

Oh, god.

She had to have been seeing things. This wasn't right. Her eyes went to the screen, to the pale hand, fingers raised to the ceiling, as if clawing for something above.

No. Still there. It was real, as real as the crystal glass just a hair away from his fingertips . . .

Stifling the scream in her throat, she looked down at her own glass, then dropped it like it was on fire, wiping the spilled wine from her hand on her dress feverishly. Then she rushed for the door.

CHAPTER TEN

Diana sat in the front row of the theater, almost exactly where she'd watched *A Midsummer Night's Dream* a few hours earlier. The silent stage and empty seats around her were eerie, even with the sun sinking behind it in a cheerful pink glow. She was holding the glass of water a police officer had given her in a trembling hand, pretty sure she was never going to drink anything, again, ever.

Poisoned.

That was the word that floated in her head. Even though she didn't know it for sure, the word seemed to drift in and out of her subconscious. That, and another one.

Murder.

Marcello Camillo, the actor who'd played Peter Quince, the man who'd charmed her on the train and given her a ticket to the performance, was dead. That was obvious. If the fact that he hadn't moved a muscle the entire time she'd rushed up and down the narrow hallway, asking for help, hadn't given away the fact, it was made pretty clear now, as two EMTs carried a sheet-covered stretcher off the stage and up the staircase. As much as she tried to ignore it, she couldn't unsee Marcello's dead eyes, his pale, horror-stricken face. It was almost as if he was as shocked by it as Diana had been.

She looked down at the clear water in the plastic cup, and her stomach swam.

But she was being silly. It probably had nothing to do with the wine, or poisoning. Marcello Camillo may have looked virile and healthy, but perhaps he was masking a hidden heart condition. Or some other medical problem.

Yes, that made more sense. He was a smoker. He was likely pushing sixty. He'd been excited by the play, and boom. Heart attack.

Besides, most people never witnessed a single murder in their entire lives. Diana could remember thinking that back in Paris, when she'd seen the dead man underneath the balcony at Versailles.

Witnessing two, in just one month? That was impossible. Or very unlucky.

Though the stage itself was empty, there were plenty of police officers walking around the aisles of the theater, gathering up the other actors to interview. Diana couldn't remember who they were or what parts they played, now that they were all dressed in their regular clothing. Not that she cared much about getting her program signed now. Or at all. In fact, she was pretty sure she never wanted to see another actor, ever again.

As she was sitting there, trying to wipe her memory of the last hour, the large man with the headset came lumbering down the stairs to the stage. He threw his clipboard down with a startling clatter that echoed through the cavernous space. *"Disastro. Catastrofe!"*

Someone spoke up. "Pietro, remember to address the troupe in English. We have a few English actors here who don't speak much Italian."

Diana nearly laughed. *Disastro? Catastrofe?* It didn't take a genius to understand what he was saying, in any language. It was clear this Pietro Colombo, the director, had a bit of a temper, because he scowled and began to mutter on in Italian, his face as broad and red as a tomato.

A woman who might have played Hermia came over to him and said, very gently, "Yes, it is a terrible shock for our troupe. He was a fine actor and a good friend to us all. We will all miss Marcello very much, both personally and professionally. In the light of this, I'm not sure how we can continue—"

"Sciocchezza! We go on. No interruptions in our schedule, do you hear me! It is a full house! Every ticket sold for tomorrow! We no miss!" he shouted, so loud his voice echoed around the arena. "That is the last word! Final!"

A man in khakis and a tie, who must've been an investigator for the police force, shook his head. "We still have our investigation to do, and there's a good chance it won't be completed by tomorrow afternoon."

Pietro's dagger-eyes swung to the man. "How long?"

"Difficult to say right now."

Pietro slammed both palms on the stage, and his hefty body shook with tension. For a second, Diana felt afraid for him. Carrying all that extra weight couldn't have been good. And he was clearly so stressed out that she didn't put it past him to have a heart attack and add to the night's body count. Then he turned and scanned the actors who had gathered around them. "Then we prepare. We rehearse tomorrow with a new actor in place for Quince."

One of the men, a muscular man who Diana thought had performed as Nick Bottom, stood up. "I will take his role. *Non.* Is no problem. You see."

The director shook his head and muttered something under his breath. "*Idiota.* No. You're in too many scenes with Quince, *lo stupido.*"

Nick Bottom sat back down with a shrug. Another man, a slight man who Diana believed had played one of the fairies, said, "I'll do it."

The director rolled his eyes. "*Disastro!* All right. But we must practice. Tonight. Tomorrow. No sleep for you." He clapped his hands and started to shout orders in Italian to everyone around. The actors, all well-rehearsed in dramatic sighs, chorused their annoyance.

Diana slumped in the chair. Wasn't that the credo of the theater? *The show must go on.* Still, that seemed to apply well to broken bones or illness or bad weather. But murder? If that was even what it was. Even just an unexpected death in the cast . . . it all sounded so cold to continue on, as if Marcello hadn't meant anything or contributed anything important to the part.

Surely, his absence would be, just as Pietro Colombo had said, a disaster. But maybe thespians were used to that. And no, she didn't know him well, but he'd been part of the company for a long time. It seemed wrong to simply replace him after a three-minute conversation. He was definitely one of the best actors in the troupe.

But that was the thing. *She hadn't known him well.* Yet she'd gone ahead and created all those stupid fantasies of him, once again. And now . . . all those dreams of him possibly being something more to her seemed to disappear in her head. Just like the man in Paris. Poof. Her record on this trip wasn't exactly sterling. Men didn't just reject her. They *died* on her.

So much for *"Fall in love in Italy."*

A mustached man with a striped dress shirt and askew tie came over to her and started speaking to her in Italian. He had deep wrinkles in his forehead, and graying temples which suggested he was older, but his body was lean, with no stomach pooch whatsoever. He had a goatee, and his voice was that of a younger man. He showed her credentials, and in his picture, he looked almost like a baby. She wondered if the stress had gotten to him.

Based on the credentials, she assumed he was some part of the Verona police force, but other than that, she was lost. She simply shook her head. "No idea what you're saying."

"You're American?" he asked, stroking his goatee.

She nodded. "Yes. I'm from New York. Yes, my name is Diana St. James. No, I did not know the victim well," she volunteered, all the things they'd wanted to know about her in Paris.

He seemed taken aback by her bluntness, but quickly wrote something down. "I'm Detective Lucci. With the Verona police. I hear you find the body?"

"No. I didn't *find* him. I was with him when he died."

"Ah." He raised his eyebrows as if it was some lurid tryst they'd been in the middle of.

Diana sighed. "It was innocent, I assure you. I didn't really even know him. I met him on the train this afternoon. He sent me a note asking me to stop by his dressing room after the show. I did. He was just getting changed and he dropped dead. That's it." She set the water glass down so that she could twiddle her thumbs better.

"That's it?"

She shrugged. He seemed to be fishing for something. What else could he possibly want? Tawdry details about an affair gone wrong? "Like I said, I just met him. I barely knew him. I suppose I was just at the wrong place and the wrong time."

"Can you tell me exactly what happened from the moment you saw him?"

"Yes. I went in. He was smoking a cigarette. He said the play was terrible. I don't think he was happy with the way the other actors had performed."

"Did he mention anyone specific that he might have been having trouble with?"

"No. Then he said he had some wine. He popped the cork and offered me some but I didn't want any, at first. He told me I could help myself while he got changed, and then he went behind the screen."

"Did he seem all right to you then?"

She nodded. "Yes. He was coughing a little, but he was very animated, despite that. Sounded like smoker's cough. That's it."

"And then?"

"Then . . . he collapsed behind the screen. I went to check on him and I think he was already dead by then. He looked it, anyway; he wasn't moving at all and his eyes were open. So I turned around and called for help. That was all."

"Are you sure?"

What else are you expecting? "I don't know. It was a heart attack or something, right?" *Please tell me yes.*

The man's lips twisted. "We don't know for sure. We have to do a few tests and an autopsy. We did find a bit of residue in his wine glass that is concerning."

Her eyes went wide. "Residue?"

"Yes. There were two glasses found in the dressing room. Was one yours?"

She nodded. "I poured myself a glass. But I didn't drink it. Was there residue in both glasses?"

He ignored her question. "*You* poured yourself a glass?" He said it as if it were a crime. She nodded reluctantly. "Then those are probably your fingerprints, along with his, on the bottle."

"Yes . . . like I said, I didn't want any at first, but then I changed my mind," she said, her heart speeding up. They were fingerprinting. Collecting evidence. Interviewing witnesses. That meant . . . they were treating this as a homicide. Yes, they had to do that, until they were sure it wasn't. But she was the last person to see him alive, so that also meant that she . . . was a suspect.

Again.

"Like I said. I didn't know him. So I had no reason to . . ."

He nodded as if to say, *Not good enough. You're still a suspect.*

"And to be clear, I didn't give him the bottle of wine," she added, twiddling her thumbs like crazy now. "It was there when I got there. He said it was a gift and offered to share it with me."

"A gift? From who?"

"He didn't say." Had he said? Her mind was starting to spin. No, she didn't think so, but now, as she replayed those last moments with him, she couldn't tell what was real and what she might have just been inventing in her head. "It was just there, on the dressing room table, when I got there."

"And you were in there alone? There was no one else?"

"Yes." She nodded absently, then a thread of a memory came to her. "Oh. Well, when I got to the door, I was just about to knock when it opened, and someone came out."

"Someone?"

57

"Yes. Titania. Um . . . I'm sorry, I don't know the actress's name. She had a strange look on her face and she seemed to be in a hurry."

"A strange look? Did she look agitated?"

Diana swallowed, fully realizing what he was getting at. Had Titania brought him the wine to poison him? If she said that she had looked agitated, suspicion would fall directly on her. But that would be a lie, and she didn't want to cast suspicion on anyone. "No. Not really. I can't explain it. It was not quite a smirk, but close. She was a little distracted, I guess, and surprised to see me."

"Mariana Massari," he said quickly, pulling out a notebook and flipping back a few pages. "She said she couldn't remember the physical description, but she saw an older female as she was leaving. Must be you. Eh?"

A forgettable older female with no striking characteristics whatsoever. Yep, that's me, Diana thought sourly. "I suppose."

He read from the notebook. "She said she thought it was possible that you were carrying the bottle of wine when you arrived."

Diana's eyes went wide. So apparently, Titania didn't have the same qualms Diana had about casting suspicions around recklessly. "What? I wasn't. I couldn't even tell you what kind of wine it was."

"*Castello Rosa Vino.* Local brand, very popular around here," he said. "Well, she wasn't entirely sure if you had the bottle. She just seemed to think there was something in your hand, which might have been a bottle," the officer said with a shrug.

"No, actually, it was my . . ." She looked around, realizing she'd long since lost it. "It was my program. I was nervous, about meeting a famous actor and all, so I'd been rolling it up in my hand."

"Ah . . ." He pressed his lips together, thinking. "You say Signore Camillo invited you backstage? Are you saying he sent you a note sometime before the performance?"

She nodded, checking her purse. She couldn't find the origami invitation either. "It was on my seat after intermission. But I seem to have lost the note. It was here just a moment ago, I'm sure. It was folded. Into a flower."

She looked around her feet helplessly, knowing it wouldn't be there. Her purse was huge, and she was nervous. It was probably in there somewhere, but she had butterfingers.

He held up a hand. "Just give it to me when you find it. But in any case, I hope you weren't planning on leaving Verona anytime soon?"

"I . . ." she said, knowing exactly where this was headed. *I was, but I guess I'm not now.* She shivered. Would she be able to find a hotel around here at such short notice? "No. I'm not planning on leaving."

"Good. Could you let us know where you're staying? Because I think we're going to have a few more questions for you, if you don't mind."

Diana swallowed. She had a feeling that even if she *did* mind, it really wouldn't matter. She was a suspect, and that meant . . . questions. Police poking about. Phone calls. Suspicion. She'd been through it all before, in France.

She didn't even want to think of it, much less *deal* with all of it. She grabbed the cup of water and in one long gulp, drained the entire thing. Poisoned or not, she needed it.

CHAPTER ELEVEN

When the police questioning extravaganza finally came to an end, darkness was settling over the open-air theater, and stars were popping out overhead, dancing among the fairy lights strewn about the theater. The director was clapping his hands and shouting loudly in Italian, trying to organize the group for an impromptu rehearsal with the new Quince, and looking ever more like he was quickly heading for a heart attack. As Diana climbed the steps of the theater to head outside, a sliver of moon shone overhead, and the stars were bright in the clear sky. The silhouettes of large dark forms, maybe bats, were swooping through the darkness, giving the place an eerie feel.

So much for an exciting, romantic trip to Verona. In fact, this was pretty much the exact *opposite* of what she'd been hoping for. Creepy, macabre, sinister.

In the lobby, she spied a promotional poster for the production of *A Midsummer Night's Dream*. Titania and donkey-headed Nick Bottom took up the majority of the real estate on it, but in the corner, there was a small photograph of Quince with the other mechanicals. She leaned forward and looked closely at him, his rakish smile such a stark contrast to the expression on his face the last time she saw him.

She shuddered and pushed open the door into the cool night. Though the theater had been open-air, the specter of death had made the place stuffy and suffocating. Around her, crickets sang. She looked about the street, still bustling with people, and sighed. She'd hoped Marcello would be her guide and tell her where to go in this vast city. Now, without him, without her iPhone, she felt lost.

Remembering her girls, she reached into her purse to fish out her phone when a hand suddenly clamped on her arm.

Gasping, she looked up to see Bea. "Hi, Mommy! I love your dress! Those shoes are killer. You look so pretty! How was the play?"

Diana patted her madly beating heart and took in a breath, trying to recover from the fright as Bea and Lily hugged her. "Oh, you scared me. What are you doing here? Weren't you at the wine bar? I thought I was meeting you at—"

"That was hours ago! We were wondering where you were. The play let out a long time ago, and we—"

"What's going on here?" Lily asked, her eyes following a police officer toward his patrol car. There were three of them, actually, parked nearby, and one ambulance. "Is everything okay? Why are there police here?"

Diana held out her hands before her eldest, the worrier, could get too wound up. "Yes. Everything is fine. There was just a little bit of excitement . . . that's all."

"Excitement? Like what?"

"Someone—one of the actors—died."

Bea's eyes bulged. "Died? What happened? Like a heart attack?"

"They don't know. But of course, they had to question everyone, and—"

"They questioned everyone in the theater?" Lily asked, skeptical. "So they're suspecting foul play?"

"I suppose they are. They didn't question everyone, of course, just—"

"And they questioned you?"

"Yes. But I actually knew him. You see, I met him on the train and he was the one who gave me the ticket to the play."

Bea's mouth hung open. "Oh my gosh. How crazy! What, did he just drop dead on stage while reciting his lines, or what?"

Diana was just about done. She didn't want to talk about this ever again, though she knew, with the police on her tail, it'd be following her around every moment she spent in this town. Another town, ruined.

Stop, Diana. You'll be fine. They don't think you did it. And Verona isn't ruined. That last murder didn't ruin Paris for you. You're here on vacation with your two favorite people. It'll be great . . .

"I don't know. It's a long story. And I'm exhausted. I'm sure the police will find the answers and that will be that. Let's talk about something else."

"Great. What are we going to do? Want to get dinner?" Bea asked. "Then maybe we can walk—"

Diana sighed. "I'm actually really exhausted."

"What?" Bea's face fell. "But we came all the way up here to—"

"Yes, I know." She didn't want to tell Lily that she was a suspect in the murder and that the police had told her she needed to stay nearby. She'd have to find a hotel somewhere. Knowing Lily, she'd have a

61

conniption if she found out her mother was a suspected murderer. Bea would probably come up with all these wild theories that would make Diana's head spin even more. "I was thinking I'd stay overnight here, get a good night's sleep, and head out later."

"But Mom!" Lily protested, echoing her sister. "We came all this way to enjoy Verona, and . . ."

"Yes. I know. You're right. I'm sorry. We can get dinner."

They started to walk up the street, as Diana fished out her phone. It'd be hard to find a hotel with this thing. Her best bet would probably be to just stop at one and ask if they had room. She yawned, and stopped short as something occurred to her. "Which reminds me. Why were you two so late leaving Florence? I thought you were going to come in on the ten, but you took the two?"

"Oh, um . . ." Bea and Lily exchanged looks.

Diana didn't have to be well-rested in order to know what that meant. It meant something bad. Something they were reluctant to tell her. She braced herself as she shifted her glance between her girls. "Come, now. What is this all about?"

"Well, we—"

A horrible, eardrum-bursting giggle pierced the air, as well as the sound of heels clip-clopping on the stone walk. Diana knew that sound, as it'd been etched into her psyche. She cringed when she saw the approaching silver head and bald spot, shining in the moonlight, behind the girls.

They parted to reveal a sight she hadn't wanted to see in Verona, or Florence, or really . . . anywhere. Not a nightmare, but a nightmare come true.

It was Evan, and his lovely bride-to-be. "Hello hello hello!" he shouted, draping an arm around Bea. "How is everyone this fine evening?"

Diana stared, horrified, unable to utter a single word.

Tilda hugged herself in the chilly night air. It made sense that she was freezing, because she had little fat on her bones, and was wearing a tight halter dress that, once again, left little to the imagination. She looked up at the crumbling façade of the arena and giggled. "Oh my gawd, that place is a theater? It needs a wrecking ball to put it out of its misery, if you ask me!" She shook her head. "I bet it doesn't even have air conditioning."

Diana didn't bother to tell her it was open-air. When she finally found her voice, she said, "What are you two doing here?"

Evan smiled his most charming smile. "Well, the girls told us what they were up to, and we thought it sounded like a fun time." He looked around and nodded his approval. "This Verona place is pretty nice. Huh? Typical Italian city with typical Italian stuff."

"You don't even know what Verona is famous for," she said under her breath.

"Don't be silly. I do," Vidal said, fluffing her mane of impressive hair. "It's where *Romeo and Juliet* was filmed."

Bea put a hand in front of her face, clearly stifling a laugh. "Oh yeah? Are you a big Shakespeare fan?"

She nodded. "Huge. I love *Hamilton*. I went to see it on Broadway with some girlfriends, and I've watched it like, a thousand times on Disney." To everyone's horror, she started to rap the first few lines. A few people on the street actually turned to look at her as she jerked and spit into her hand, probably thinking she was in the midst of a seizure.

Even Evan seemed embarrassed for her, because he cut in. "Well, how about dinner?"

"One moment," Diana said, grabbing her daughters' sleeves and dragging them to the side, underneath the marquis for the theater. When she got them there, she whispered, "What in the world were you thinking?"

Bea frowned. "I'm sorry, Mom. We both are. We tried to lose him. We did. We only told him where we were going right before we were about to leave. We never thought they'd follow us."

Lily nodded. "But then they rented a car and showed up here! Can you believe it?" She looked over her shoulder at them. "I think Vidal put him up to it. I swear, that witch has got something up her sleeve."

Bea snorted. "She doesn't wear sleeves. Or any clothes at all, really." Then she looked back at her father and leaned in. "But Mom, I don't know about Daddy. He's acting kind of weird and desperate. I almost feel sorry for him, having to put up with Vidal. It's like he's smiling, but in the back of his mind he's wondering what the hell he was thinking."

Diana dragged her hands down her face. That wasn't her problem to solve. He'd made that bed. Now, she really was too exhausted to think. "Whatever. I'm just going to find myself a nice hotel and take a nice hot bath and decompress."

"Hotel?" She must've spoken too loudly, because Evan barged in, leaning into their circle. "No need. We just rented a huge villa right outside of town. Right, Tilly? Sleeps fourteen. There's plenty of room for all of us."

Tilda looked less than thrilled. She checked her manicure. "Well, Evan, I didn't know we'd have company. I thought you and I would—"

"Nonsense. We'll have plenty of alone time. The place is huge. It has a pool, a gym, and it's supposed to be in a vineyard. Lots of room for us to spread out." He gazed at Diana hopefully.

Bea clapped her hands. "Perfect. Lead the way. As long as I don't have to pay for it, I'm in." She looked at Diana hopefully, and in those sad puppy-dog eyes, Diana could almost see the little four-year-old who needed Mommy to kiss all her bumps and bruises.

"Yeah, Mom. We've hardly seen you. At least we can catch up at the villa?" Lily said.

"Well . . ." she said, even though at this point, the idea of finding a hotel was almost less appetizing than marinating in her ex's company. What if she couldn't find a place? Besides, at least the girls would be there. And they were gazing at her hopefully. She hadn't seen Bea in so long. She really wanted nothing more than to spend time with them. "I don't want to be a thorn in your side, tagging along like that . . ." *Like you've been.*

"Nonsense. There's a chef there, preparing dinner as we speak. I can just add on an extra person. And I have a car. We can all squeeze in together!"

Diana winced. The five of them, in a little Italian clown car? This was almost worse than their jaunt to Disney World years ago. And yet another dinner where Vidal would likely get drunk and insult her phone another twelve thousand times? Torture. She was about to decline when Vidal bopped forward, gazing at the poster on the side of the wall for the play.

"Oh! *A Midsummer Night's Dream!* I know that show. Isn't that the raunchy one with all the sex? And the rockin' soundtrack?"

Diana exchanged glances with her daughters. Evan cleared his throat. "I wouldn't know. I've never been much of a William Shakespeare fan. Never quite understood it in school."

Vidal rolled her eyes. "Oh, honey. You should be! He was amazing. The way he came up with those turns of phrase like that? It was like, I don't know! Like poetry. Supposedly, he invented it." She started to rap *Hamilton* again, this time with spittle flying everywhere.

Seriously, on this Earth, there could be no worse or more cringeworthy performance.

This time, Bea really did burst out laughing. "She is *definitely* throwing away her shot."

Diana grabbed her and led her away before Vidal could notice. "Fine. Let's just go. Lead the way."

They only got a few steps before the door to the theater opened, and Detective Lucci appeared. Diana did her best to sidestep him and pretend she had no idea who he was, but he stopped right in front of her, making ignoring him impossible.

"Signora St. James," he said directly, not looking at any of her companions. "Did you find that note from the deceased yet?"

"Oh, um . . . yes, I think I did find it," She opened her purse again, rummaging around until she pulled it out, with a few more creases than it had had going in. But it was still very much in the shape of a flower, with *Princess Diana* written neatly upon the front. As she handed it over, she could feel the wide-eyed gazes of her family on her. "Here you go."

"Thanks," he said, opening the flap and peering at it. He spun to leave, his black dress shoes squeaking underneath him, but stopped suddenly. "Remember. Stay close. You have an address yet?"

She started to shake her head when Evan spoke up. He held up his phone. "Yes. One-twenty Via Del Pestrino. We've got it rented for the next three days."

"And after that?"

Diana winced. "I guess I'll have to find a hotel. But I will keep you updated."

She could feel the questioning looks of her family all around her, as the detective nodded. "Good," he said, and headed to his patrol car.

He'd hardly been gone a second when Bea and Lily asked, in unison, "What was that all about?"

"It was nothing, really, it was—"

"You had a note from the dead guy?" Lily said, grabbing her arm and shaking it a little. "Why did you have a note from him? That's evidence!"

"Mom? What did that note say?" Bea asked, latching onto her other arm and shaking it, too. She felt a little like a martini.

"Stop," she said, nudging them loose. "It was really nothing much at all . . ."

"It was in the shape of a rose!" Lily said. "And now the guy's dead. That was nothing?"

"Di, let me try to understand something. That policeman wanting you to stay in town . . . Does all this commotion around here have something to do with you?" Evan asked, his brow wrinkled in concern, looking around at the police cars.

Tilda let out a shrill giggle and batted her eyelashes at a couple of burly police officers at the entrance. "Oh my *gawd*, it does look like CSI around here!" she said, as though she'd just noticed the police cars. Then she started to sing-song, *"Diana's in trouble! Diana's in trouble!"*

She giggled more, but no one joined in. For once, Diana didn't mind it, because it took the attention off her. But as soon as Vidal fell silent, her daughters and Evan swung their gazes back to Diana, like a pendulum.

Diana sighed. "Like I said, it was nothing. I met him on the train. He gave me the ticket to the show, and invited me backstage after the performance." She paused, not wanting to go on, because a man dying in her presence was certainly *not* nothing. There was no way she could spin it that way.

"Mommy. Are you saying a dashing actor invited you backstage? Like a groupie?" Bea's cheeks were red in awe.

"A *dead* actor," she reminded her. "And no. I wasn't a *groupie*. Far from it. I barely knew the man. I was—"

"But he died before you could go back there, huh?" Evan asked, crossing his arms.

Diana winced. *What is he trying to be, my babysitter? Maybe he should babysit Vidal before she breaks out rapping again.* But as goofy as Evan could be, he had a way of asking the revealing questions.

"Not exactly." They were still all staring at her, expectant, so she decided to just get it over with. Rip off the Band-aid. "He died in the dressing room while I was there. The police think there might be foul play, that he might have been poisoned."

"Poisoned?" everyone said in unison.

In the resulting silence, they all just stared at her. Even the crickets seemed to quiet. Despite the chill, Diana felt flushed.

Vidal spoke up. "Oh, *gawd.* Did you do it?"

Now everyone stared at her.

"Of course she didn't." Evan put his hand out, touching Diana's forearm. She stiffened as he said, "Well, don't worry, love. We'll stand by you. To the very end."

Vidal scowled, for the briefest of moments, then erupted in a shrill laugh. "Wow, Diana, you really *are* in trouble, aren't you?"

Diana sighed. Yes, she assumed she was in trouble. And now if she wanted to escape this dysfunctional family reunion before she self-destructed, it was probably up to her to figure out how to get out of it.

CHAPTER TWELVE

The clown car ride was even more horrific than Diana had expected.

Really, Diana decided it could've only been made worse if Vidal decided to entertain them with her rapping skills again. Vidal did, however, put on some music that sounded like a cow giving birth. Diana and her daughters had squished into the back seat like sardines, and the car seemed to lack any suspension, so every bump on the unpaved road toward the house shot straight up Diana's spine.

Luckily, the place wasn't far out of town. A few miles later, Evan turned onto a long dirt driveway and exclaimed, "Ah! Here we are."

Diana craned her neck to see in the dark a large building, awash in the light of what looked like gas lamps. The place was on a riverbank, overlooking the main part of town, a magnificent, three-story sandstone masterpiece with terracotta roof and arched doorways, leading to a wide courtyard with a stone fountain. The windows were covered with sea-blue hurricane shutters, but were wide open, likely giving expansive views of the town.

Diana let out a little wistful sigh as they approached. It was a place like she'd dreamed. Too bad she had to share it with Vidal. Well, Evan may be a fool, but he did have a certain amount of taste when it came to luxury.

Stirring her from her dreams, Vidal let out a horrible giggle, grabbing Evan by the arm. "Oooh! It's so pretty! I'm going to spend all day tomorrow on a lounge chair by the pool with a fruity drink, working on my tan."

That was one place Diana was sure *not* to be.

It might have been a place like Diana dreamed, but this? This felt like a nightmare. Being so close to the people that, in part, she'd gone halfway around the world to get away from? She couldn't miss the gentlemanly way Evan pranced over to the passenger side and helped Tilda out of the car, while she herself crawled out of the small opening from the back seat, nearly stumbling on the uneven cobblestone as she tried to gain her balance. Tilda fixed her dress and went inside without even bothering to think about her bags, leaving the rest of them to struggle with their luggage.

Evan gave Diana a sheepish look. "It will be nice, eh? All of us together?"

Lily looked at Diana and muttered, "In what alternate universe is he living?" When Diana smiled, she added, "Are you going to be okay with this, Mom?"

Diana nodded. "Don't worry, darling. I'm an adult. I can handle myself."

She hoped, at least. She really didn't have much of a choice.

But as she grabbed her bag and trundled inside, she realized Evan was right in one respect. The place was huge. If she *did* want to avoid the happy couple, it shouldn't be too hard. She turned to go up the long, sweeping staircase with the wrought-iron scrollwork railing, when she caught sight of a giant table, set for five. The smell of garlic and onion wafted up to greet her. It smelled lovely, but Diana had other things on her mind.

Evan came out of the room and clapped his hands. "I spoke with Gaia, our housekeeper. She says dinner will be ready in five minutes. She's making *Pastisada de caval* . . . it's a specialty of Verona, a traditional horse meat stew!"

Bea groaned. "That's evil."

Diana hadn't felt sick to her stomach before, but now she was getting there. She looked longingly up the stairs, then shook her head. "I really think I'll just call it a night."

"Mommy!" Bea said, pouting, like only the youngest in the family could. "Why? Don't you want to have dinner with us?"

She shook her head. "I don't think so. I'll just . . ." She trailed off as she pointed upstairs.

This time, no one stopped her, but they did all watch her as she climbed the steps. As she reached the top of the landing, Evan called, "Tillie took the master bedroom. But feel free to take any other one!"

The hallway stretched in front of her, full of rooms. As she trudged along it, she yawned, the exertion of the day catching up with her. Hopefully, she'd be so tired that despite all the worries on her head, she'd sleep like a rock.

She peeked in the first few rooms. Small bedrooms, some with twin beds, some with full, all covered in plain blankets. Then she noticed a massive room with a high, wood-beamed ceiling and king bed. A gaudy pink suitcase, something Barbie would tote around, had been set on the bed. She didn't need three guesses to know who that belonged to. She went across the hall, finding the room at the end of it, and pushed the door open. Even if there was a den of spiders in there, even if it was haunted by the former owners, she was prepared to claim it as her own.

But as she turned on the light, she smiled. It was a lovely, large room with an en suite bath. She went to the open windows and peered out at the stone courtyard, bordered by olive trees. The fountain made a calming gurgling noise as she leaned out over the railing, taking in the night air. She could do this. Be here, with them, while navigating the Marcello situation, and not lose her mind.

She *had* to do this.

"Mommy?"

She turned around to see Bea standing in the doorway. "Yes, dear?"

Bea came in and sat on the bed, hugging herself. "Are you okay? You seem so . . . far away. And I don't think it's just because of the horsemeat stew."

She managed a smile. "I'm fine. Really. Just tired. You should go down and enjoy dinner. Don't worry about me."

The worry lines didn't disappear from her youngest's freckled brow. "I don't know if you should be alone after what happened. It must've been terrible to see that man die."

"Yes, it was. But—"

"And I know Dad probably isn't the person you want to be with, right now. But still . . . we're here. Don't forget us."

Diana sat on the other side of the bed and touched her youngest's hand. "I know. I'm sorry. You're right. I probably shouldn't be alone. But—"

"I get it. Not with *them*." Bea motioned downstairs.

Diana nodded. "I promise we'll do something tomorrow. I've missed you so much, darling."

Bea sniffled. "I did, too."

It was surprising for Bea to reveal such a thing. Lily may have been older, but she was the needier one, always looking for Mom's opinion on things. Bea was the adventurer, the fearless one. She often barreled into things, trailblazed, did things on her own. She wasn't ever one to admit she was lonely. "Honey. What's wrong?"

Her daughter's smile was bright, but obviously fake. "Nothing. What do you mean?"

"There's something else. Besides me. Come now, you can tell me."

She smiled sadly. "I don't know. I guess you could say that Hai was being a little distant before I left. He didn't even seem to care that I was going on this trip. I get the feeling he wants to break up with me."

"Oh, come here," Diana said, pulling her into a hug. "Maybe he's just preoccupied. Have you spoken to him since you left?"

"I've tried calling him, but he's been too busy. I just—" She stopped and pulled away. "I'm sorry, Mom. You are probably right. I'm just overreacting. Besides, you have enough on your plate. You don't need my problems, too."

"No, that's not—"

"Seriously. It's okay." She wiped her cheek. "I'm fine. What are you going to do about the police? I can't believe they would think you have something to do with it."

"Yes, but—"

"You really think he was murdered? Who could've—"

"I have no idea. They're running tests. But I suppose they think it could be murder. And I have no idea who else could've done it. Probably someone in the play. They don't let just anyone back there."

She hugged herself. "How horrible. You can't leave here until they clear your name? Really?"

Diana shrugged. "It's standard procedure, Bea. And I'll be fine. It's nothing for you to worry about. So just go downstairs and enjoy your time in Verona. All right? Catch up with your sister and dad, and I'll see you tomorrow." She pointed to the bathroom. "I'm going to take a nice bath. It's calling to me."

Bea nodded. "All right, Mom. We can catch up tomorrow? Maybe do some sightseeing?"

"Of course. It's a date. In the afternoon? I have a couple things to take care of in the morning."

"Ha, Mom. You know I don't like to wake up until noon, anyway, on my vacations."

Diana smiled, got up, hugged her daughter again, and closed the door behind her. Then she went to the bathroom and flipped on the light to find a giant clawfoot tub, big enough for two. She ran the warm water, found a vial of bubble bath under the sink, and poured the pink liquid in until it started to froth and fill the air a with a sweet-smelling lavender fragrance. Just what she needed.

71

Though she doubted anything could wash away the worries on her mind.

*

The night air had been crisp and cool, but not cold. Pleasant. The sheets had been new, but soft to the touch and smelled of detergent. The pillows and mattress were plush and luxurious, like a cloud. The song of crickets melding with the bubbling of the fountain was a comforting lullaby. The other rooms of the house were so far away that not a peep could be heard in the outside hallway, not even Tilda's horrible laugh. There had been nothing at all to disturb her; even when the sun began to filter in at dawn, it came up on the other side of the house, so its rays hadn't bothered her.

So everything should've been in order for a good night's sleep.

And yet Diana hadn't slept at all. Not for one minute.

All she'd done, all night long, until she'd nearly gone mad, was compile question after question about the murder of Marcello. *If* it was even a murder.

Now, it was time to get some answers.

She rolled out of bed as the sun was dawning on the green hills in the distance, and changed into her clothes from the day before. Gathering her things into her bag, she stepped outside and went down the darkened hallway. At the bottom of the stairs, she ran into the housekeeper, Gaia, a plump, grandmotherly lady with a wide smile. She said, too loudly for Diana's liking, "Ah! You must be Signora Diana? I am sorry I did not meet you last night. Breakfast for you?"

"Ah, no," she whispered, pointing to the door. "I have to—"

"I have made fresh bread. It is still warm. And I have my homemade jam. Cappuccino?"

Diana paused. That sounded *good.* Not only that, the smell coming out of the kitchen was heavenly. After eating nothing last night, her stomach was begging to be put out of its misery. "Can you make that to-go for me?"

She nodded and motioned her into the kitchen. "You have someplace to be? May I call you a taxi?"

"Oh, no, that's not necessary. I think I'd rather walk to town and enjoy the weather."

72

"Ah, yes. Beautiful day! But please, be careful. We are on a hill. The walk can be dangerous and steep."

Diana grabbed a slice of crusty bread and slathered it with peach preserves while Gaia poured her a commuter cup of coffee. When she was ready, Gaia accompanied her to the door and opened it for her.

"Be careful, Signora St. James. Have a lovely day exploring our city!"

I hope so. "Thank you . . . uh. Could you tell me the direction for the theater, so I can get my bearings?"

The woman pointed down the street. Diana squinted. None of it looked familiar. Her fingers itched for her iPhone, but she squared her shoulders and said, "Perfect. I hope you have a great day as well."

Diana meandered downhill, toward the rapidly rushing green-tinged river. Yes, the pathway was steep, and it was dirt, so her feet slipped on the loose gravel several times, and she almost fell twice. Once she got to the edge of the river, she found a small stone bridge and a walking path, winding along the banks. She stopped at a picnic table on St. Peter's Hill, overlooking the town, took a bracing sip of the hot cappuccino, and gazed past the wide Adige River, at the many orange roofs, majestic red-brick towers, and church spires of the hillside town. The winding streets were mostly empty, the sign of a sleepy, relaxed place that had yet to wake. She took a deep breath, trying to enjoy the calm of the beautiful day.

But her mind dragged her back to those tense moments inside the dressing room, when she'd gazed upon Marcello's dead body. His eyes, wide with fear and confusion. She shuddered.

If it was murder, then it was poisoning. If it was poisoning, then the wine was the method. That seemed obvious.

But why? What had he done to make someone want to murder him? And who had given him the wine?

Titania. Or Mariana Massari, as Detective Lucci had called her. She seemed like the most likely suspect, since she'd been in the room right before Diana. But that didn't mean she'd brought him the wine. Really, anyone backstage could have given it as a gift to him.

Actually, *anyone* could have, whether they'd been backstage or not. Marcello had had all those cards and gifts from admirers scattered around his dressing room. A bottle of wine could've been left at the stage door for him. Isn't that what admirers usually did when they had gifts for actors they wanted to pay respects to? Maybe it was just some crazed fan.

Diana squinted as the bright sun came up, cresting a copse of cypresses behind her, with their delicate green-yellow leaves blowing in the breeze. The day was growing ever warmer, so she shed her light sweater and tied it around her waist. Too many possible suspects. This was not going to be easy for the police to figure out.

That means . . . Diana, you might as well get comfortable here.

She winced at the thought of being imprisoned in the villa with her ex and Vidal for months on end. Surely, she'd go mad by then.

Closing her eyes, she forced herself to think. A lot of people may have had the opportunity to give him the wine, yes. But who had the motive?

She really didn't know Marcello well enough to know that. The only person who came to mind was the actor who played Nick Bottom. He'd been almost too eager to volunteer to take on his role. Any role. And something about him had rubbed Diana the wrong way. He'd seemed a little full of himself. Maybe he'd wanted Marcello's role for himself. But resorting to murder to get it? That sounded a little extreme.

As for other people with motive, well, jealousy and drama ran deep in the theater. Plus, she couldn't put it past a crazed fan.

So, in terms of narrowing it down, that . . . really didn't help at all.

What she needed was to get back to the theater. To ask around at the scene of the crime. Maybe she could find the person at the stage door and see if he remembered the wine bottle being delivered to Marcello. Yes. And stagehands and crew members usually knew all the gossip that went on behind the scenes. They'd be a wealth of information.

She checked her phone. It was just about nine o'clock. The theater was probably already buzzing, getting ready for their afternoon performance of *A Midsummer Night's Dream*, if the police hadn't put the kibosh on it. Even if it was cancelled, the director Pietro had seemed pretty adamant about conducting more rehearsals. The theater would likely be full of people she could question.

Standing up, she hurried down the path toward the Arena di Verona. If she got there early enough, maybe she could get these answers and clear some things up.

CHAPTER THIRTEEN

Though the drive to the villa the previous night hadn't taken very long, it turned out that the walk back to the theater wasn't an easy one, even though mostly downhill. The path was unpaved, and Diana got a rock in her shoe that she couldn't find, though she kept stopping every so often to shake it out. Even though Gaia's directions had seemed pretty straightforward, she got a little lost on all the narrow streets, since so many of the buildings looked the same, with their stone-washed exteriors and orange roofs. By the time she got to the Arena di Verona, she had a blister on her heel.

She finished her cup of cappuccino and tossed it in the trash as she approached the front doors. Unfortunately, when she tugged on the front door, it was locked. There was a sign on the front door in Italian that she couldn't understand, but she imagined it said something about the performance being delayed.

Frowning, she cupped her hands around her eyes and peered through the glass. The place was dark.

So much for them being up, bright and early, preparing and rehearsing for the next performance.

She looked around, wondering what she should do next, and then turned back to the arena. If she didn't find a way in there, she was at a dead end. She might as well go back to the villa and spend time with Evan and Vidal.

And she *really* didn't want to do that.

She wandered to the side of the theater, where the massive, crumbling stone ruins arced around, nearly coming in contact with a row of small houses, bisecting it. There was only a narrow alley between them, with a set of stairs heading downward on the hillside. It didn't look like a very heavily traveled route, but as she neared it, she wondered if it would lead to a back entrance.

Before she could think better of it, Diana stole across to it and slipped between the buildings, descending the stairs as fast as her blistered foot would allow.

When she got to the bottom of the steps, she noticed a set of rusting double metal doors in the façade of the building. One appeared to be wedged open an inch or two.

Checking both ways and seeing no one, she wedged her fingers in the opening, pried the door open, and slipped inside.

She blinked, trying to adjust to the darkness. That familiar smell of mold from the weeping walls returned as she looked around, spotting a few empty costume racks, light fixtures, and clothing trunks. One block wall was covered with framed posters from other performances— *Othello, Romeo & Juliet, Hamlet, Much Ado About Nothing, The Taming of the Shrew.* Diana's eyes caught on a photograph of Marcello, wearing a ruff and holding Yorick's skull, in the Hamlet poster, his mouth shaping the words, "Alas, poor Yorick!"

He'd played Hamlet. What a talent.

Marcello. Now dead. Murdered, probably, in this very building.

Shivering, she climbed a short staircase and found herself in the hallway with the dressing rooms. To her left was the one belonging to Marcello. His name was still scrawled upon the chalkboard.

Just what she was looking for.

The only problem was, there was some yellow crime-scene tape across it. Not *really* a problem. She could simply push it aside, something that was made much easier since the *Do not cross* part of it was in Italian. She could just pretend she didn't understand it.

If she dared . . .

Did she? In any language, this was illegal. And she'd gotten into a few not-quite-legal scrapes in Paris. Luckily, she'd finessed her way out of them, or else she might never have left France. But it was only a matter of time before her luck ran out . . .

She imagined Vidal, laughing at her in that high-pitched way. *Diana's in trouble!* she'd screeched. Even the memory of it was enough to shred her eardrums.

Wincing, she took a deep breath. She'd just put her hand on the doorknob when she heard a voice call out in Italian, behind her. She jumped and whirled to find another dark hallway, rimmed with curtains. After a few yards, though, this one widened up. Beyond another curtain was the stage.

She took a tentative step toward it, pushing aside the simple black curtains as she moved through. "Hello?"

"Hello?" a male voice called back, as uncertain as her own.

She stepped forward, away from the curtains, and found herself on the stage, which was empty, and looked much larger from this standpoint. Scanning to the seats, she noticed a young man with a close-cropped haircut and a gray jumpsuit, standing near the orchestra pit. He was picking at his teeth with his fingernail and leaning up against a push-broom. "The place is closed," he said when she appeared, not unkindly. "How did you get in?"

She pointed behind her. "Sorry. The door was open."

"I leave it open. To get air through. Smells like stink here, otherwise." He motioned her back. "You're not an actor or a part of the crew. That means you shouldn't be here."

"Oh, but I—"

"You selling something? Doesn't matter. You shouldn't be here anyway. The police told me to keep anyone out. It's a crime scene. You come to see the show?" He checked his watch. "Might not even have a show today. Police might not let us. They're still investigating."

"I didn't come to see the show. I saw it yesterday, though."

"Did you? Then you know why the police don't want anyone here."

Diana looked for a way off the stage, and finding a set of stairs to the side of the curtain, went over and descended until she was at eye-level with the man. "I understand. Were you here yesterday, too?"

"Yes. One of two stagehands they got. Me and the old man, Berto. I mind the area behind the stage, set things up, and clean the place when everything's done. Wasn't able to do it last night because the rehearsal ran late. And the police don't want me touching certain things in the back." He eyed her curiously. "You didn't touch anything, did you?"

She shook her head. "Just the door, when I opened it."

He sighed, went to the cupholder on one of the near seats in the front row, and picked up a bottle of water. Taking a long gulp, he shook his head. "Hard to believe Camillo is dead. I don't get what happened."

"Could've been a heart attack?"

He shook his head. "That's all to stop people from freaking out. What I heard, and what the police have been saying, is that it's murder. Someone poisoned his wine. And you didn't hear it from me, but I think a jilted lover had a hand in it. He was always one for the ladies."

"Is that right?"

He nodded.

"So you clean up in the back? You cleaned their rooms, right? Where do you think that wine would've come from? Did an admirer leave it at the stage door for him?"

"That's just it. I don't know. The man was very popular. He got lots of gifts, and I was the one to go to the stage door to get them. Lots of lady admirers. But not wine. Not that I can remember. Usually he got candy. Cards with lots of hearts on them. Romantic things." He leaned forward and whispered, "*Undergarments.*"

Diana's eyes went wide. Undergarments? Really?

"Maybe Berto knows. He usually waits at the entrance from the lobby. He's older though. He don't remember so good, and don't speak English very good, either." He shrugged.

That was probably the uniformed man she'd seen before she went backstage the previous day. "Did you see the wine in the dressing room at all, like when you were cleaning up in there?"

He shook his head. "Not that I remember. I cleaned the night before. If it came, it came the day of the performance. Either by one of the actors or crew, or it was left at the front with Berto. That's the best I can tell you."

"And where is Berto?"

He checked his watch. "He won't be in for another few hours. He sleeps in after performances."

Okay, this wasn't producing any concrete information. She decided to switch her line of questioning. "It *is* crazy. I just wonder who would do such a thing. Do you have any clue who'd want to murder him?"

He started to shake his head, then gazed at her, eyes narrowed. "Why are you asking so many questions? Are you one of those armchair detective types? Nah, you don't look like one. But if you are, I don't think you should be here. Pietro wouldn't like it. He told me to keep everyone else out and only clean up in the theater."

"Oh. No." Thinking fast, she said, "I'm actually a friend of Marcello. Well, an acquaintance. He invited me to the play. And I'm just so shocked. I want answers. For him. For his family. He deserves them."

Sympathy flooded the man's eyes, and his shoulders slumped. "I know. I feel the same. He was a good man. Most of the actors, they don't care for us little people. But Marcello was kind. He should not have had this happen to him. I guess . . ." As if suddenly remembering, he reached into his pocket and pulled something out. It was a silver apple on a keychain. "He bought this for me. From his trip to New York. Gave it to me yesterday. He was always thinking about us."

Diana smiled. "That's nice. I heard about his trip to New York for the audition."

"Yes. He was a good actor. One of the best. I think if anyone was angry or jealous of him, it would've been the other actors. They weren't as good as he was. Maybe they had enough of him. Or the ladies. He had quite an eye for them." He grinned at her, his expression suddenly wolfish. "I bet he had an eye for you. You look like his type."

Diana fought the blush on her cheeks. "Like I said, I didn't know him well. He just invited me to see the play. So, you think other actors were jealous of him?"

"Definitely. He was good at what he did. You should've seen him in *Hamlet*. Brought the house down in the title role. He won an award for it."

Now, this had definite potential. "Really? So . . .Which actors would you say might have been jealous?"

He shrugged. "I don't know. All of them? But in a competitive way. I'd never think in a murdering way."

Okay, that wasn't helpful. Diana thought back to right after the murder, when the Nick Bottom actor had jumped at the chance to play Quince. That was kind of odd, that he would be so ready to fill his place, so over-eager, almost as if he'd been planning for that moment to pounce and take over. Maybe this was all part of his diabolical plan to get the role he really wanted. "What about the actor who played Nick Bottom?"

"Luca?" He shrugged. "Nah. Not Luca. Or . . . I don't know. Yes, he was very angry last night, but Luca's a gentle soul. Kind of goofy. He couldn't hurt a fly."

"He was angry last night?"

"Yes. Or more like hurt and embarrassed, I think. He kept asking Pietro, our director, to play another role and he stormed out when he was turned down, after asking about a dozen times. He's not a very good actor, in my opinion, though he thinks he is, so Pietro was right." He laughed. "You know, he was acting like himself. Nick Bottom. That's the only person he can play well . . . an ass."

She smiled. So he knew the play well, too. The irony hadn't been lost on her, that the actor who played silly and self-important Nick

79

Bottom wanted more important roles in the play, since that's exactly what Nick Bottom had wanted in *A Midsummer Night's Dream.*

"But I think Luca and Marcello got along well. I thought of them as thick as thieves. But I don't know. I didn't know any of them all that well. Just enough to say hello to. Certainly not well enough to think any one of them would stoop to something so terrible. I cannot believe that any of them could've done such a thing."

"But the police think someone did? You really do think they're leaning toward murder?"

He nodded sadly. "Yes . . . I keep thinking that it has to have been an accident, or a heart attack. At least, that's what I want it to be. I don't want to face the fact that it could be one of the company."

"What about Titania?" Diana blurted.

"Mariana?" He smiled with a touch of dreaminess. "Oh, she is wonderful. She's a very famous actress in these parts. A celebrity. Grew up right in town here, down the street from my aunt. She left for many years to travel in the theater, then she comes back. Everyone loves Mariana."

Clearly, he did, too. "Did she get along well with Marcello?" She thought back to what Marcello had said once. "They both grew up here, right?"

He shrugged. "Yes. I think the two of them, they got along very well. As far as I know. I see them talking together. They were both very kind people. Such a shame."

Diana sighed, frustrated. According to this guy, *everyone* in the theater was so wonderful. She was getting nowhere. "Yes, it is. Do you—"

Suddenly, the back door opened up with a crash, and the hulking director, Pietro, came plodding down the staggered steps from the back of the arena, toward them, clipboard in hand.

He stopped about three steps in and looked up from whatever he was reading. Even from across the arena, Diana could see the narrowing of his eyes. She braced herself.

"You!" he shouted, his words echoing, and then he began screaming something in Italian. *"Cristoforo!"* He motioned to the stagehand and then to Diana, shouting all the while.

The stagehand, whose name Diana gathered was Cristoforo, gave her a nervous look. "He says you're not supposed to be here, so I think you should probably go . . ."

Diana took a step forward, preparing to leave. "I understand. Thank you," she said, as the director continued to scream, gesturing so wildly with his face so red, the heart attack once again looked imminent. "I appreciate your—"

Cristoforo suddenly took a giant step back, as if she was infected. When she looked up at him, his eyes were wide with a combination of horror and revulsion. "He says he thinks *you* killed Marcello?"

Diana's own eyes went wide, but with shock. "Me? Of course no—"

"He says you were in the room with him when he died? That you put the poison in his glass and the police are almost certain it's you?" The stagehand suddenly wheeled on her, gripping his push-broom in two hands, like a weapon he was ready to slash at her.

"That's not true," she said, backing away and holding up her hands in defense. "Not at all. I just came here to get some answers because I know it wasn't—"

But clearly trying to tell them anything wasn't going to work. They were advancing on her, getting ready to pounce, as if she were some common criminal. Pietro pulled out his phone and started to jab in a number. Probably the police. She moved another step backwards, nearly stripping over the first step of the stairs to the stage. Turning quickly, she rushed up them, heading for the backstage door as fast as she could.

She only stopped for a second, to pick up a dog-eared copy of the play program, which had been discarded on the floor in the back room.

When she was again on the street, she took a deep breath, trying to calm herself. *This is not good. They think I'm the murderer. The police think I'm a murderer.*

She opened the program to the cast of characters. Right over Marcello's picture was that of the rather square-faced, tan, and muscular man who played Nick Bottom . . . Luca Castille.

At least she had a name. Now, if she wanted to stop these crazy rumors from flying around and save herself, she had to find the man. And she'd have to look—anywhere but here.

CHAPTER FOURTEEN

Though Diana didn't know the town or language of Verona at all well, and though she didn't have the latest model iPhone to help with her efforts, finding the address of Luca Castille proved to be far less difficult than she'd expected.

All she had to do was stop in at the café, down the street from the theater.

It had been pure luck. After she ran away from the director and stagehand, tail between her legs, she found herself with an incredible thirst. So she'd stopped in there, hoping to rest her blistered foot and get something to drink. But as she looked around the small, busy place, she smiled.

The café was practically *devoted* to the actors of the theater. Made sense, since it was called Caffè Al Teatro. Every available space on the wall was taken up by theater posters and other memorabilia. The same Hamlet poster from the theater took up prime real estate in the seating area. The counter itself was fashioned to look like a replica of the arena. Behind the counter were signed portraits of many of famous actors, and not-so-famous ones, too. As she was paying for her bottle of San Pellegrino, her eyes caught on a picture of Marcello. Right next to him, there was one of the man of the hour, the man she wanted to see—Luca Castille.

She looked up at the young, tattooed barista and said, "Luca Castille, huh? Does he come in here often?"

The man looked over his shoulder. "*Si.* Before every rehearsal and performance. A lot of actors do."

"You see him in *A Midsummer Night's Dream*? He was amazing."

The man gave her a look that said, *Whatever. I just work here.* "I don't go to plays."

Makes sense why you work here, then. "Oh. But . . . Luca obviously loves this place, considering he comes here all the time, huh?"

He shrugged. "I don't know."

"I saw him," another barista, a middle-aged woman with long blue-tipped hair and a surprising American accent, said. "He's okay."

"You're American?"

She nodded. "New Jersey! You?"

"New York!"

"Hey, neighbor. But I moved here a decade ago. Luca's really good, but Marcello . . ." She fanned her face. "That man who plays Oberon in that latest production could light my panties on fire."

Diana debated whether this was the right time to tell her that Marcello played Quince, not Oberon, and that he was dead. "Yes, he was very good, too. So you saw it last night?"

She shook her head. "But I heard about it. I've seen all the other ones. Soon. Maybe today."

"Did Marcello come here often, too?"

She nodded. "Luca most of all, though, since he lives right upstairs."

Diana blinked, hardly believing her luck. "Upstairs? So are you saying there's like, an apartment building up there, and Luca Castille lives there?"

She nodded. "Yep. Right upstairs. He's down here almost every morning."

The male barista closed the register and dropped the change in Diana's hand, wordlessly shrugging, like, *You got your coffee. Now be off and leave us alone, lady.*

"Thanks," she said, twisting the cap on her bottle and taking a much-needed swig. When she went outside, she went to the right of the narrow building, finding only an alley with a bunch of trash cans in it. Then she went to the left. There was a long, straight metal staircase attached to the side of the building, leading up to a landing with three doors.

One out of three. I'll take those odds, she thought, her shoes pinging on the staircase as she climbed. The thing was mostly rust, and swayed a little as she climbed, making her worried it might collapse underneath her. She held tight to the railing, saying a prayer of thanks when she stepped onto the solid concrete landing.

She knocked on the first door she came to, the middle one, and waited.

No answer.

Giving up, she went to the one closest to the street. She knocked, and again, got the same result. She checked her phone. It wasn't too early, but it was the middle of the day. People with regular nine-to-five

83

jobs probably weren't at home. Actors, though? He'd probably gotten home late last night, from the rehearsal. Maybe he was out. Or already at the theater. Was it possible that she'd walked right past him, on her way here?

Almost ready to call it a day, she knocked half-heartedly on the last door.

It opened almost immediately, revealing the handsome, scruffy face of Nick Bottom himself. Door open only a crack, he eyed her suspiciously, wordlessly.

"Luca Castille?"

His eyes narrowed more. "*Si* . . ."

"Hi, um . . . you probably don't recognize me, but I was there at the theater, yesterday, and—" She paused as he continued to eye her, uncomprehending. His eyes slipped to the play program in her hand, and he let out a little sigh, like he wanted her to get to the point. "You do speak English, yes?"

He nodded and ran a hand through his scruffy hair. "Yeah, but I don't sign autographs here, and really don't appreciate the interruption. Who told you I lived here? You can catch me at the stage door an hour prior to—"

"No, I'm not looking for your autograph," she said, almost too readily, because suddenly he began staring at her with a bit of contempt, as if to say, *Why don't you want my autograph?* She quickly backtracked. "I mean, I saw the performance yesterday and I did think you were enormously talented, but I am a friend of—"

He scratched the back of his head and yawned so loudly, it broke her train of thought. "Look, I'm a little busy. Could you please get to the point? What are you looking for?"

"It's about Marcello. I was his . . . friend. He invited me to the performance yesterday."

At that, the man's eyes widened a bit. With guilt? "Are you with the police? I told them everything I had to say. I don't have anything more."

"No. I'm not. I'm a friend of his, that's all. And I heard the police think it could be murder, that he was poisoned, and I just want answers. Can I come in? I have a few questions. That's all."

He looked behind him, then started to open the door wider. As he did, a male voice said something to him in Italian. He responded in a tired voice and stepped aside to the smell of food cooking.

It was only when Diana was inside the small apartment that she realized that Luca was only wearing a towel around his waist. His muscular body was like that of a professional weightlifter's—cut and completely hairless. She averted her eyes as he motioned to a chair in the living area.

The place was surprisingly neat and modern, a stark difference to the crumbling exterior. It was painted a cheerful light blue with art-deco furnishings, and on the wall were a few large, Andy Warhol–style paintings of Luca, in coordinating color schemes. As she lowered herself into a bright yellow plastic chair, part of a retro kitchenette, she saw the other man, who was just as lacking in the clothing department, standing in front of a sizzling pan on the stove. He had on a pair of tight underwear and an apron, and was holding a spatula.

She decided her best course of action was to look down at the floor. It was wooden, and absolutely spotless and shiny, like that of a bowling alley.

"What did you say your name was?" Luca asked her as she fought the furious blush on her cheeks.

"I'm Diana St. James."

He sat on down across from her. "Diana. This is David."

She looked up. David smiled at her and wiggled he fingers in a wave. It was the perfect name for him, because he almost looked like that statue of David replica she'd seen in Florence—pale, lean, with abundant curls, and, of course, nearly naked. "Oh. Hi."

"*Euvo e pancetta?*"

Diana's eyes shifted to Luca's. "Um . . ."

"Bacon and eggs," he explained. "David makes the best of them."

"Oh. No thank you. You speak English very well."

He nodded, unimpressed with himself. "Yes. Most of us actors do as we take on jobs all over Europe. David here doesn't speak a word of it, so I apologize if he doesn't say much." He smiled adoringly at David, who smiled back. He shrugged. "David is blissfully ignorant to everything we discuss, which is why I adore him. I like things uncomplicated."

David winked at her.

With that, she now *completely* lost her train of thought once again, until David came and set a mug on the coaster in front of him. Luca dragged the mug toward him and leaned in close, taking a large sniff.

"I'd offer you something to drink, but it looks like you have that covered." He rolled a hemp coaster over to her. "You had questions?"

She placed her bottle of San Pellegrino on the coaster. "Ah, yes. I did. I—"

"Wait . . ." He was back to eyeing her suspiciously again. "You were the one in his dressing room when he died. Right? I remember you being there afterwards when the police were questioning us all. And the dress. Blue. Right?"

She nodded. "Good memory."

He shrugged. "Great dress. Custom? From that little boutique downtown, right? *Piazza Bra,* yes?"

"Yes. Thank you. I was really shocked by his death, as you can imagine. And now the police think it's murder. I can't get it out of my mind."

"I can imagine. Did he just drop dead in front of you?"

She nodded. "Pretty much. One moment he was talking to me, drinking wine and getting changed, and the next moment, he'd passed out dead on the floor. It was very scary. And I was just wondering if you had any idea who could've done something like that?"

He shook his head, wiped his brow with his hand. "No. I can't. It's shocking to me, too." He looked over at David, who nodded. "I came home and told David, last night, and we just . . . couldn't believe it. Not Marcello. We both had ourselves a big cry."

"You knew Marcello well?"

He nodded. "I did. David knew him from my association with him. He was a gem. One of my best friends. In fact, he brought me into the *Compagnia del Andre.* We—"

"*Compagnia del—?*"

"*Andre.* That's our troupe. We do all types of Shakespeare productions, at least six a year. It's the most respected one in all of Verona, maybe even the area. We're all like family."

"And every actor in the play yesterday was part of the troupe?"

He nodded. "The major roles, at least. The minor roles might go to other people outside the troupe. We are all very close, and we respect each other greatly."

This wasn't leading to any good information, either. From everything she'd heard, everything seemed to be sunshine and rainbows in the troupe. That didn't explain a dead body. She needed to change her tack. "I saw that you offered to play his role, after he died?"

He nodded. "Of course. He and I—we run lines together all the time. So I know the Peter Quince part better than anyone. We all know each other's lines well, because we often trade parts. So obviously Pietro had other plans." He made a face.

"You don't like Pietro?"

He exchanged a knowing glance with David. "Not particularly. His opinions are too strong, and he doesn't listen to anyone else. The man's an obese, bull-headed fool, if you ask me. But he's our leader, in charge of all the decisions, so I grin and bear it so I have a job. If he don't like me. . ." He slashed a finger across his neck. "I don't agree with much he's said, especially with the latest production. Terrible."

"So you weren't happy with the performance yesterday?"

He laughed. "Were you? I thought it was a horror. No chemistry. No spark."

Diana smiled. Maybe she would've had a better idea on what was missing if she'd been able to speak the language and understand what they were saying. "I liked it. I'm by no means a theater expert, though, but I could tell there was talent with you all."

"Some of us, more than others?" He asked with a wink. He rolled his eyes. "Pietro has, in the past, made some questionable decisions on who he takes into the company. We all think so. But at least, under his direction, they learn. I'll give him that."

"I didn't notice. I thought you were all very talented."

"Perhaps. But there is more to a production than good acting. It's a certain kind of magic that can't always be captured." He glanced at David again, then leaned back, stretching his arms over his head and flexing his muscles. He looked down at himself in admiration. "It's the way the different players interact, a chemistry that doesn't always translate well on the stage. This production was a *dog* to plod through."

"Oh. What do you mean? So some of you didn't get along?"

"There was—how shall I say it?" He tented his fingers in front of him. "Tension. Between a few of us."

"Marcello? And . . ."

"Mariana. Definitely."

"You mean, the woman who played Titania? What makes you say that?"

He smiled. "Just a hunch."

"So they weren't friends?"

87

David came over with a plate of eggs and slabs of cooked *pancetta*, which he set in front of Luca. It looked really good. Luca smiled up at him and squeezed his hand. "Wonderful, *grazie,* David." He picked up his fork. "Oh, they were friends. Like I said, we all were. I think of everyone, Mariana and Marcello created the most fireworks. They were bickering constantly. Probably because they knew each other too well. Grew up together, went to school together, you know. Very close. Almost too close."

"Is that so?" Diana asked, deep in thought. Maybe there was something there. She had left his room with a strange look on her face that day. "You saw them fighting? Before his death?"

"No. Never fighting. Bickering. And when I say bickering, I mean they were just back and forth. Almost teasing each other, sometimes rudely. You know, like brothers and sisters do. But I think it was starting to get on Mariana's nerves, to tell you the truth. Maybe that is why she asked me to switch. She didn't want to be near him for all those scenes that Titania needs to be near Nick Bottom—too hard for her to be close to him."

Right, because in *A Midsummer Night's Dream,* Titania, put under a love spell by Oberon, the king of the fairies, falls in love with Nick Bottom, whose head had been changed to that of a donkey's, by the mischievous sprite Puck. So there are quite a few love scenes. "She asked you to switch?"

"Oh, yes. A few weeks ago, before our rehearsals started. I auditioned for and was set to play Quince. It was a role I'd played before, in university. I thought I was better suited for it. But Mariana Massari is a big name, even bigger than Marcello Camillo. She spoke to Pietro, and he had the roles switched. So I got Nick Bottom. I was shocked. Marcello enjoyed the comic parts, so he was suited to it. I'd never done comedy in my life. But me? I like to stretch. So I said yes."

Diana's eyes widened. "And what did Marcello think about this sudden change?"

"Like I said, it's normal for switches to happen, even though some of us are better suited to roles than others. If he was upset, he never let on. That wasn't Marcello's way. I've never seen the man angry. Most actors are dramatic and emotional, but not Marcello. He was, how you say, happy-go-lucky. He never showed the angry side of himself, with anyone, as far as I knew." His lips twisted. "But I did overhear him saying something, a couple days ago, that did surprise me."

"What?"

"Well, I was walking to my dressing room after a rehearsal, and I had to pass his. I don't know who he was talking to, but it might have been Pietro, when he told Marcello that she wanted the roles switched. I'd never heard him sound quite so serious. It almost sounded like a threat. He said, 'That is the mark of an evil person, stooping so low, taking something from someone like that. Mark my words. I don't let people like that off easily.'"

Diana played that over and over again in her head. "You think he was upset with Mariana?"

He shrugged. "I don't know. When all of us were around, he was so lighthearted. He teased Mariana that she didn't want to act in scenes with all of his manliness, things like that. He made fun of her. As always. But when he said that, I thought, hmm. Maybe Marcello has a darker side he doesn't reveal to others so easily."

"Stooping so low. I don't let people like that off easily," she repeated, almost to herself. Had he and Mariana quarreled, until she thought the only solution was murder? "Was she angry at him for making fun of her?"

He nodded. "Probably. She's a bit of a prima donna, that one. Likes things just so. And she liked to dish it out, but she couldn't take it so well."

"So she asked Pietro to change the roles," Diana said, more to herself. "But did she tell you that was why she wanted to make the switch?"

He shrugged. "She told me she thought she and I would have more chemistry, and that it would make the play work better. Guess that tells you who's the better actor." Then he burst out laughing and slammed a fist down on the table. "I'm joking, of course. But nevertheless, that's what she said. And how could I turn her down? Nick Bottom's a great part. Looks good on my resume, for sure."

"Oh, for sure. So . . . you really don't actually have an idea who could've done this to Marcello?"

"Not Mariana, if that's what you're getting at. She's too sweet."

There it is again. Everyone loving everyone in the theater. They are definitely good actors.

"So there was no one acting strangely, prior?"

"We're actors. We *all* act strangely, dear. It's when we're acting normally that you have to worry about us." He shook his head, and his

89

eyes turned downcast. "It's terrible. I really can't believe anyone would do something like this. Marcello didn't have enemies. He got along with everyone. But then I think about what he said . . . and I have to wonder."

The stagehand had said he got along with everyone, too. But maybe that was only one of many characters Marcello Camillo played. Maybe he did have a dark side. But if so, why was he dead? "What was he like?"

"Big flirt. Ladies' man. He lived for the women. In fact, it was a running joke for him. He didn't want any of the other men in the troupe getting more female admirers than he had. It was almost an obsession for him, to amass his posse of groupies. He was always looking out for them. He wanted them all to himself." He laughed. "But he was serious about none of them."

Great, Diana. You fell for another lothario, hook, line, and sinker. Rather than dwell on it, she decided to change the subject. "So you didn't see where the poisoned wine came from?"

He shook his head. "I never even saw the wine. I didn't see Marcello all day, except for on the stage. I told the police this. Why are you going around asking the same questions?" He didn't seem angry, only curious. "You say you're a friend of Marcello's?"

"Just an acquaintance, really. But he was kind to me when I met him on the train. Offered me that ticket. I suppose he was just trying to add me to his legions of female admirers. But I feel terrible about what happened," she said honestly. "Tell me, does he have any family in the area?"

Luca shook his head. "He told me he was an only child, and his parents died years ago. No wife, obviously. I don't even believe he ever had a serious girlfriend." He shrugged. "The closest thing he'd have to family around here is Mariana. Like I said, they were close."

Diana thought he'd say that. "I'd like to ask her some questions, too. Do you happen to know where she lives?"

"Yes. Ponte Nuovo, near Piazza Bra."

This was where Diana would type the information into her phone. Lacking that, she rummaged through her purse for a paper and pen. Not finding that, she looked around helplessly. "Um . . ."

He motioned to David, and shouted, *"Mi serve carta e penna!"*

David approached with a pen and a piece of note paper and Luca quickly scribbled something down, which he slid across the table to her. He tapped it as she read it: *2719 Via Ponte Nuovo.*

"That's where she lives. It's a couple blocks from the Piazza." He smiled. "Be careful, though."

"What do you mean?"

"She may be sweet to those she knows. But she's not very fond of outsiders. Especially women. She likes to be the belle of the ball, so you say." He grinned. "Though she be but little, she is fierce."

Diana didn't like the sound of that, but she really didn't have any choice. "Thank you."

"Don't mention it. You might be able to catch her there. Or she'll be at the theater later. We're supposed to be there at noon."

After what had happened that morning, Diana wasn't sure she *ever* wanted to go back to the theater. She looked at the paper. Without her phone, it'd be like finding a needle in a haystack. "Think you can draw me a map of it, so I don't get lost? I don't have my phone, and . . ."

Amused, before she could finish, he took it back and drew her the map. "You really can't miss it. It's right at the entrance to the Shakespeare Festival, so follow the crowds and you'll find it." Then he passed it over to her. He dug into his eggs as she stood up. "Good luck."

David smiled at her as he opened the door for her. "*Buona fortuna,*" he said to her as she went through.

Outside, she almost forgot how shaky and precarious those metal stairs were, until they started to shake as she raced down them. Holding tight to the railing, she navigated carefully down them, and picked up the pace.

Maybe Titania, the queen of the fairies, could sprinkle her pixie dust and give her more answers than she'd gotten so far.

CHAPTER FIFTEEN

As Diana headed down the street toward Titania's address—at least, she thought she was heading toward the address, but it was impossible to tell without GPS—her phone buzzed with a call from Lily.

"Mom! Where are you?" Lily asked when she answered.

Diana cradled the flip phone between her shoulder and her ear as she turned the map Luca had drawn in her hands. Nothing looked like the gridwork of streets around her. She needed a compass. A guardian angel. *Something.* "I'm fine. I—"

"You disappeared and we haven't seen you. Gaia said you left even before breakfast! We were worried about you. Are you all right?"

"I'm sorry, darling. I thought—" Diana stopped walking, confused. Then it suddenly made sense. She'd only told Bea of her plans to be busy in the morning. "Is Bea still sleeping?"

Lily paused. "Yes. She said it was jet lag, but I don't buy it. She's the *worst* in the mornings. Like the wicked witch. She actually threw a shoe at me when I went into her room to wake her. What is she, like, still twelve?"

"Oh. Well, she was probably the last person I should've counted on to relay the message. But I told her that I had some things to do this morning."

"Some things to do? Like what?"

"Just errands. You know. Annoying things you wouldn't be interested in," she fudged, since she really couldn't think of any errand that made sense. "But I told Bea I thought we could go sightseeing later."

Lily sighed. "Later? What about now? Dad's freaking out about you."

Diana's eyes went wide. "He is? Well, it's not like he's my warden or—"

"Yes, but I am, too. After what happened at that theater, with that actor being murdered? That's really creepy. You really shouldn't be alone with some murderer running around town. You never know what could happen."

Uh-oh. Lily had been talking to her father. When the two of them got together, they let their minds wander to crazy scenarios. In Lily's world, just about everyone was a possible axe murderer. "Oh, honey, but I'm absolutely in no danger whatso—"

"And Dad said that the next time that detective tries anything with you, he's going to call his lawyer. That's no way to treat an American."

Diana scoffed. So he still felt he needed to watch over her, even though he'd been the one to officially end their marriage? Like she was some incompetent child that would fall apart without his assistance. She couldn't keep the bitterness out of her voice. "Oh. Like I said. I'm fine. I was fine. And I'll be fine, with or without him!"

There was a pause. In that pause, Diana could sense that Lily didn't believe her. "We were going to town to have lunch at the Shakespeare Festival. Why don't you meet us?"

Diana looked up at a street sign. She'd expected it to be Via Camillo, but it wasn't. It was Via Barone. Great. What was north, and what was south? The sun was high in the sky, so that wasn't helping. She'd gotten herself all turned around. Worse, the sweat from her hand was starting to blur all the ink from the directions, and now she had no idea what arrows were pointing where. "Yes. Sure. I think."

"You think?"

At that moment, she wasn't sure she'd even be able to find her way back to the house. Titania's house was supposed to be near the Shakespeare Festival, but there were no signs of it around at all. No people heading in that direction, no music wafting over the buildings. She spun, finding the hill the house was supposedly on . . . or was it? Much like the buildings, all the hills looked suspiciously alike. Where was the river? "I actually think I'm a little lost. Without my GPS . . ."

Lily laughed. "Go to a street corner and tell me where you are. We're getting in the car in a few minutes. We'll pick you up."

"We? You mean . . . you and Bea?" she asked, hopeful.

Her voice was low. "I just woke up Bea, so of course Bea, and . . . the others."

"The others?" She cringed.

"You know I can't shake them. They're like glue."

93

Wonderful. He's probably going to spend the entire time harping on how terrible my sense of direction is and how I shouldn't be alone in this city. And then he's REALLY going to be stuck to me like glue.

She let out a breath of air. At least the festival would likely be crowded, and she and the girls might be able to give them the slip. "All right. Barone and Castillo."

She couldn't put them off any longer. She had to spend some time with them, after all. So this was as good a time as any. And, since Titania's home was so close to the Shakespeare Festival, maybe she could kill two birds with one stone.

*

"Oh my *gawd*, how stinkin' cute is this place?" Tilda exclaimed as they walked toward the crowds of the fair. It was taking place in the historic part of the city, surrounding the main piazza, with booths set up along the narrow street, selling everything from crafts to food. Costumed actors walked about, playing instruments or acting out parts of Shakespeare's plays. Jubilant flute and lyre music from the Elizabethan period played. It was like a walk back in time.

Except that it was very hard to totally immerse oneself in the history and culture with Vidal constantly pulling out her phone to take selfies of her and Evan next to every single sight, and saying, "I bet you miss taking selfies, huh, Diana, with that totally Jurassic phone of yours?"

Diana hung back and exchanged glances with her girls as Tilda took a picture of Evan with some poor, hapless Lady Macbeth impersonator who'd happened to cross her path.

When Tilda was finally satisfied with the photo, she squealed. "This is going on my Insta-feed! I look so good!"

Evan immediately looked at Diana. "Don't get lost now." He smirked.

She scowled and glanced at her oldest child, who shrugged innocently. Of course Lily had told him that she'd been lost in Verona earlier. Now, he'd never let Diana live that down. "I'm perfectly capable of making my way through a strange city without a phone. It might take me a little longer, but that's fine. There was a time when phones didn't accompany us everywhere we went, in case you've forgotten!"

Tilda finished sending off her social media post and began admiring a rack of brightly colored scarves. Watching her drape one over her neck, he leaned into Diana. "I'm sure you are capable, but are *you* forgetting that you just witnessed what could be a murder? And the murderer can still be out there. What happened to you last night, at that theater, had to have been harrowing."

"Yes, it was. But I'm fine."

He chuckled. "You say that, Di. But I know you. I know how when the smallest thing doesn't go to plan, it sends you into a tailspin. You may be good at thinking on your feet in the business world, but in life? I saw your life flash before your eyes when that detective approached you. And you, being in a strange city, in a strange country, without your phone? You must be—"

"Again, I'm fine. Of course it was a shock, but I'm a grown woman." *Which is less than can be said for your intended.* She crossed her arms, watching Tilda giggle as she draped a scarf over her head like fifties starlet. She donned dark sunglasses and assumed a duckface for the mirror. "And I am not your responsibility anymore, am I?"

"Di. I'll always feel some responsibility for you. I care about you. I want you to be happy."

"Did you think that following me around on my vacation was going to make me happy?" she asked, as Tilda suddenly noticed Evan wasn't by her side. She looked around for him, frantic, and her eyes narrowed when she saw exactly where he was. "Because as happy as I am to see the girls, I don't really find very much joy in—"

At that moment, Tilda stalked up to him and grabbed him by the arm. "Come on, Evan," she said, glaring at Diana. "There's a booth up here selling these goofy caps with feathers in them. I think you'd be totally dashing in one, Ev!"

It was almost as if she'd been talking to a wall. He gave Diana a goofy shrug and let himself be pulled away by the young girl. *I might as well just save my breath,* she thought. *He is never going to get it.*

The happy couple walked ahead, Tilda glued possessively to Evan's side, allowing Diana, Bea, and Lily to linger far behind. Thank goodness. She didn't need him as her warden. To put even more space between them, she stopped at a stand, admiring blown-glass sculptures that sparkled in the abundant sunlight.

"These are pretty," Diana said, holding up one of Romeo and Juliet. "Don't you think?"

Bea wrinkled her nose. "It's okay. Not my thing. So did you get everything done that you had to, Mom? All your *errands*?"

She said that last word in a way that said she didn't believe her, either. Diana nodded. "As best I could."

Up ahead, Tilda was fitting the most hideous floppy feathered cap on Evan's head. He was looking in the mirror, tilting his head this way and that. *Oh, god. He's actually considering buying that monstrosity.* Bea said, "Bet it's hard, not having GPS in a strange city."

Why was everyone in her family so hyped up on that? It wasn't like she'd lost a leg.

"Oh, yes," Diana tore her eyes away from the train wreck that was soon to be Evan's most recent purchase and laughed. "I actually had to look at street signs and ask strangers. The horror."

"When is your phone coming in?" Lily asked, picking up a glass sculpture of a fish.

"I don't know. It was on backorder, but they said they'd call me when it was ready. Hopefully, I can have it shipped to me before I leave here."

"This one," Bea said, holding a many-colored glass sculpture up for inspection. "This one is perfect for Vidal."

They all looked at it. It was a sculpture of a large, fat woman, singing. She had a lot of hair and a revealing dress that showed all of her many curves. It was hideous.

They all burst out laughing.

"Oh, yes. I'm getting this sucker for them as their wedding gift," Bea said with a smile of satisfaction. "It can go right on the mantel of their tackily decorated house."

"How do you know it's going to be tacky? Maybe Tilda has good taste in décor," Diana said, trying to give her the benefit of the doubt.

"Um. Mom. She actually wants to wear a Dalmatian-print wedding gown. Or zebra. She's not sure. She just knows she wants animal print."

Diana winced. "Oh. That's bad."

"You have no idea. Luckily, we're not her bridesmaids!" Lily said, glancing at Bea, who nodded.

Bea said, "Yet. She hasn't asked us."

Diana smiled as she set the ugly sculpture down. "Did they set a date yet?"

"I think Vidal wants a Christmas wedding. She was talking about getting married somewhere in the city, spending all of Dad's money in her ugly gown," Lily said with a groan. "Last I heard, her guest list had five hundred on it. And that was just her side."

Diana winced again. Poor Evan. This was a far cry from the small, intimate ceremony they'd preferred. He was such a love-blinded fool, wrapped around Tilda's finger. He'd entertain her with whatever whims Tilda had in a way he'd never entertained Diana. But he seemed to be having a delightful time doing it, so it was none of her business. "I'm sure it'll be fun. I'll still be in Europe."

"No, you're not!" Bea shouted, jiggling her arm again. "You're coming! I don't care if they don't invite you and I have to drag you all the way across the Atlantic to come as my guest, Mom. If we have to stand it, so do you."

"And don't forget. I'm due in December, remember?" Lily said, patting her stomach. "So you might be in town for that. Though I wouldn't mind missing the wedding of those two lovebirds myself."

They stopped by another booth with lots of traditional, handmade baby clothes, with adorable hand-stitched smocking and embroidered accents. Diana picked one up; a pantsuit with a little sailboat on the collar. "This is perfect. For a boy or a girl. I have to buy it for you."

Lily smiled. "Thanks, Mom."

She handed the clerk the euros, tucked the package under Lily's arm, and they walked a little farther. As they did, Diana took notice of the numbers. Sure enough, 2719 Via Ponte Nuovo, Titania's address, was right behind a stand selling gelato. Diana scraped her teeth over her bottom lip. She *had* to get there.

"Oh, good, we lost them," Bea said with a wink, searching through the crowds.

Stirred from her thoughts, Diana looked around. Sure enough, Evan and Tilda had completely disappeared into the throngs of people. She couldn't say she minded that at all.

"Want to get food?" Bea asked as they came to a green area scattered with picnic tables.

Since the last thing she'd had to eat was the bread and jam at Gaia's, Diana was hungry, but she had other things on her mind now. She said, "Why don't you girls go ahead? I forgot something."

Bea's pert nose wrinkled. "You . . . forgot something?"

She nodded. "Yes . . ." She blurted out the first thing that came to her. "I realized I didn't get an engagement present for Tilda and Evan. I feel terrible."

"Don't feel *too* terrible," Lily mumbled. "They probably haven't noticed, considering."

"Even so. I saw something back there I really think they'd like." She pointed vaguely behind her.

"That statue! I'm telling you!" Bea said, eyes gleaming.

Lily sat down at a table under an umbrella, claiming it for her own. "I am starving. Baby's starving. He's screaming, *Feed me!* This is serious."

Bea nodded. "I'll get you something. Do you want us to get you something, Mom? I'm getting pizza. Do they sell pizza in Italy?"

Diana, distracted, answered, "Oh, fine. Just get me one of whatever you're getting. Thanks. I'll be back soon!"

She dashed off into the crowd, scooted behind the gelato stand, and ran down a charming alley full of tightly packed together homes, with plants on the doorsteps and wrought-iron balconies, from which some people had hung their laundry. She would've stopped to admire it, but she was in a rush. By the time she climbed the steps to the front stoop of Titania's house, her foot pinched at little. Was she getting another blister? Out of breath, she rang the doorbell.

A moment later, a woman answered. Even without makeup and costume, this woman was not Mariana Massari. She was elderly, very tall, and frail, with a short gray bob and pale, tissue-paper skin. "*Si?*"

"*Ciao* . . . I was looking for Mariana Massari?"

The woman shook her head. "No. She go to work. I keep house for her."

"Oh. She went to the theater?"

The woman shrugged. "I guess. I don't ask. Come back later."

A dead end. Diana looked around as the woman closed the door on her. It was too much to go back to the theater now, especially with her girls waiting for her. Besides, in this busy town, without a map, she wasn't sure she'd ever find the theater again.

So maybe Evan was right. Maybe she *couldn't* do this all on her own.

Her shoulders threatened to slump, but she held them back. No. She *would* do this. She'd have to make plans to get to the theater as soon as possible, once her sightseeing excursion with the family was over.

Diana checked her watch. She'd only been gone five minutes. There was still plenty of time to pick up some engagement gift at one of the tables and arrive back at the food court without making the girls worry. Maybe it was good that Titania wasn't there. She'd had enough of third degree from her family; she didn't know if she could handle much more lying. Maybe she should just try not to worry about the murder, trust the police were taking care of things, and enjoy being with her family as much as possible, while they were still in town.

This time, instead of walking down the busy concourse between the booths, she stuck close to the sidewalk, where there were fewer people. She passed a small bookstore, a hardware shop, and a café, all of which had their doors open to welcome fair attendees.

At the corner of the block, she noticed a familiar logo, a rose within a triangle. She gazed at the logo, thinking, *Why does that look so familiar?*

She stopped, trying to remember where she'd seen it. She peered in the window of the shop to see high-top tables, a bar, and rows upon rows of wine bottles, stacked up behind the counter. A wine bar.

The answer came to her almost immediately: She'd seen that logo on the poisoned bottle of wine in Marcello's dressing room.

CHAPTER SIXTEEN

She glanced at the sign. Castello Rosa Vino—Sala Degustazione. So that was where the poisoned wine had come from. Hesitating, she let curiosity win out.

Forgetting everything else, she stepped through the open door.

The place was full of people, all sitting at tables, tasting tiny flute of wine. All of them seemed relatively healthy and unpoisoned. Had she been thinking she'd see more victims dropping dead at her feet, the result of a bad batch of grapes? She looked around, wondering just *what* she expected to find here. Someone in the back room, adding poison to the bottles? A health inspector, coming in and condemning the place for selling tainted wine? It seemed hopeless.

Maybe, though, someone had sold a bottle to someone who worked at the theater. She had to at least try to talk to someone who worked there.

Making her way through the crowds, she stepped up to the bar, keeping an eye out for anything suspicious. She was so busy checking out the bottles on the wall that she didn't notice the bartender until she stood right in front of her.

When Diana did focus on her, she gasped with recognition.

It was Titania.

No, she wasn't wearing her makeup and costume, but there was no doubt. She'd recognize that small stature, those high cheekbones and bright eyes anywhere.

"Come posso aiutarti?" the woman asked expectantly.

"Titania? I mean, uh, Mariana Massari?" Diana blurted.

"Si . . ." The woman eyed her doubtfully.

Diana simply stared until more and more doubt leaked into the woman's face. She seemed almost angry. "Oh. Um. I'm sorry," Diana said, remembering. "You work here, in this place?"

She nodded, her face showing no recognition of Diana whatsoever. It was clear she *really* hadn't gotten a good look at Diana during passing, outside Marcello's door. "Who are you?"

"My name is Diana St. James. I was at your performance yesterday. *A Midsummer Night's Dream*. I didn't know you worked here."

She scoffed. "Well, in case you didn't know, being an actor doesn't pay the bills." She looked around. "But this is my family's place. I help out when I can."

Her family's place. And here she was, saying she'd never seen the wine. *Liar*.

Mariana studied Diana. "I feel like I have seen you before . . .?" Suddenly, her eyes widened. It was about time. "You're—"

"Yes. I'm the person who went into the dressing room after you. You told the police that you thought I had a bottle of wine when I went into see Marcello. You knew that wasn't true," Diana said, wagging her finger at her. As she did, people on either side of her turned to look.

Mariana looked around, now worried. "I didn't—"

"Yes, you did. That's why they think I had something to do with this."

"Come." She motioned Diana to follow her. Diana hesitated, wondering whether it was a good idea to follow a potential murderer into a room alone. But the place was crowded. She wouldn't try something, here. At least, Diana didn't think so. Taking a deep breath, she walked around the bar and followed her into a back room, which had an impressive floor-to-ceiling collection of wine bottles.

The moment Mariana turned around, she'd clearly recovered from whatever guilt she'd had, because her face was a deep scowl. "Oh, and it has nothing to do with you being in his dressing room when he died? Listen, you *cagna*. Something happened to him, and I had absolutely nothing to do with it. It kills me to know that there is some murderer out there, who took his life."

"So you're saying you didn't bring him the wine?"

She hesitated. "Well . . ."

Diana crossed her arms. "Well, what? If you didn't bring it, you must at least know who bought it from this place."

Mariana let out a deep sigh and rolled her eyes to the ceiling. "All right. I did bring it to him. It was just a gift. He loves a glass of wine after a performance. But I didn't poison it. Of course not. Marcello is one of my oldest and dearest friends." Her voice cracked, and she leaned her elbows on the bar. "It's hard to believe he is dead."

Great. She was putting on the waterworks now, too. First, Luca's tears, now this. And they all seemed so genuine, so emotionally distraught about the loss of this man. Diana guessed that kind of sensitivity went with the territory of being an actor. But was it sensitivity . . . or was it a bunch of bull? How would she be able to find out who was lying? "Yes. Very sad. When did you bring him the wine?"

"Before the show, of course. I didn't do it often, but I had done it a couple times before. It was in his dressing room the whole time, and Marcello wasn't in there once he got his costume and makeup on. So I think—"

"It means that just about anyone could've poisoned it."

Mariana nodded. "Well, anyone who had backstage access. That is dozens of people. But I have a hard time believing anyone could do that. We're all like family."

That was the same thing Luca had said. No one believed anyone was capable of this. And yet, someone had done it. At least she'd narrowed down the list somewhat, removing the possibility of it being a crazed fan. It was definitely someone in the troupe, or one of the actors or stage crew who helped out in the performances.

"What I don't understand is how the wine could've been poisoned prior to the cork being popped. I saw him pop the cork. Is it possible something was in the glass that he didn't notice?"

She shook her head. "Not true. You can remove a cork with a lighter, and seal it up easy, no problem." She motioned her forward, to a metal prep table, and grabbed a bottle of wine from the rack. "I'll show you."

She reached into her pocket and pulled out a lighter. Igniting it, she carefully held the flame up to the neck of the glass, turning the bottle at its base. After a moment, the cork did begin to move, climbing up, higher and higher in the throat of the bottle, until suddenly, *Pop!* The thing flew up to the ceiling like a popped champagne cork. Diana covered her head, but the cork fell to the ground on the other side of the table and rolled away.

"Wow," Diana said. "I didn't know that."

"A lot of people do, though," she said defensively. "It's not much of a secret. Maybe the murderer did, too."

Yes, you know it. And that means you might be the murderer, Diana thought. But then again, if it could implicate her further, why would she be demonstrating it to Diana and announcing the fact?

She studied the bottle. "And you can stuff the cork right back in, after putting the poison in?"

"It is not easy, but it can be done." Mariana smiled sadly, and Diana saw something in her eyes. A fragility that would be hard to fake. "And Marcello wasn't the most observant of men. He would maybe not have noticed if someone played with the cork."

"Mariana, can I ask you something?" Diana asked as they both stared at the bottle of the wine between them. "Luca, the man who played Nick, said that Marcello was originally set to play Nick Bottom, and you asked the director to make the change. Is that true?"

She nodded.

"Why?"

She shrugged and her eyes didn't meet Diana's. "I simply thought Luca would be the better actor."

That was a lie. She might have been a good actress, but she wasn't that good. "It had nothing to do with your feelings for Marcello?"

She began to shake her head, but finally let out a long exhale. "Fine. I was in love with Marcello. I always have been. I don't think it's much of a secret now." She shook her head. "He's never led me on. Not at all. He was not the type. In the play, Titania is put under a spell where she falls in love with Nick Bottom when he sings and showers her affections upon him. I didn't want to do it. Not only would being so close to him make me fall even deeper . . . it felt too much like real life. Unrequited love is too painful. I can't even act it, these days, now, without losing it."

"Oh. I see."

"So yes, I asked Pietro to switch the roles, and he obliged. I don't think Marcello minded much. Like I said, though he knew the way I felt, he never pretended, not even for a moment, that he returned my affections."

She wiped a tear from her eye and smiled.

Diana said, "You need to tell the police this."

Her eyes widened and she backed away. "Oh, no. I couldn't do that."

"But you have to. They're going to find out about the wine anyway. It'll look better for you if you come forward and tell them, rather than having them seek you out."

"No. I can't do that. Maybe they will find out about the wine, maybe not. But I don't want to put any bad publicity on my family's place. Anyway, it doesn't matter what they find, because I am not the one who poisoned it. So let them dig around me as much as they want. They will find nothing to sink their teeth into." She shrugged. "I am up for a major part in Roma. A feature film. My star is on the rise, finally, after all these years. I am not going to jeopardize that by inviting the police to come sniffing at my door."

"So you're just going to have them continue to sniff at mine?"

She gave Diana a once-over, then shrugged as if to say, *Better you than me. As plain as you are, you likely have nothing in your pathetic little life that would get ruined.*

"*I'll* tell them."

"Fine. Do it. I have nothing to hide. They come for me now. They come for me later. What is the difference? It is of no matter to me."

But it matters to me, Diana thought. *I can't get out of this town until my name is cleared.*

Mariana went to a cabinet, pulled down two glasses, and poured two glasses of rosé wine. She offered one to Diana, who took it. Thinking of Marcello, she had no interest in drinking any of it. Mariana held up her glass. "*Salud,*" she said with a small smile, taking a sip. "If you are innocent, you have nothing to worry about. Let them keep sniffing and eventually they will move on."

Diana blinked. *But what if they don't? What if they decide I'm guilty?*

She couldn't just let it sit still. She needed to keep digging herself. But where?

As she walked to the door, the idea solidified in her mind . . . The place she'd find the answers was probably the only place in town where she was absolutely unwelcome.

CHAPTER SEVENTEEN

Diana left the tasting room, her head spinning.

As real as her tears over Marcello had been, if Mariana truly was innocent, then wouldn't she, like Diana, be doing everything possible to try to prove it? And if she had information that could lead to capturing the killer, wouldn't she come forward and give it to the police? Why was she hanging back . . . simply because of her career?

It just made her look more guilty.

Diana came to edge of the curb and stepped onto the street, so deep in thought that she almost had her toes run over by a festival vendor with a food cart. *Scusi!"* he called, tipping an imaginary hat at her.

"It's all right," she murmured, wondering if she should go to the police and rat on Mariana. It was only fitting. It was the truth. And regardless of what Mariana did, she had a responsibility to share what she knew.

So why had Mariana brought the wine? Just as a gesture of goodwill? If she knew Marcello wouldn't return her affections, what was the reason? Was she hoping to finally persuade him, change his mind? That seemed doubtful. But then, why else bring a bottle of wine to an unrequited love? Maybe she was jealous. Maybe her insane jealousy had driven her mad. She had the motive. The opportunity. She knew how to open the bottle without a trace. Yes, she was the best suspect, for sure. Maybe Titania's fingerprints were on the bottle.

Of course, if they were, they were probably mingling with Diana's own fingerprints, since she'd poured herself a glass. Neither set would really prove anything. And . . .

Diana's knees wobbled as a thought came to her.

What if she'd taken a sip of the wine?

She'd been so close. She'd raised it to her lips, intending to drink. It was only her nervousness, her curiosity about the room, and trying to carry on a conversation with Marcello that had prevented her from taking that first sip.

Oh my god. I could've been dead, too. This could've been a double murder. I could've been going back to America in a casket.

Maybe Evan was right. Maybe she really couldn't take care of herself alone in a strange country.

The severity of the situation and the thought of her own mortality came crashing down around her, making it hard to breathe.

Just then, a person on a bicycle dinged his bell at her. She jumped out of the way and moved under the shade of the building's overhang. She needed to think. To breathe.

As she stood there, thoughts came together in her mind. If Mariana had gone there with the wine, maybe it was just to share it with him. Maybe she was just hoping that he'd drink it with her. And if so, that didn't make her a likely suspect. She hadn't looked nervous when she left the room . . . only a bit flustered. Surely, if she'd had murder in her heart, she'd have been showing more emotion than that?

But really . . . to use wine from her own family's vineyard to poison a man? She wasn't stupid. She had to have known that method of murder would've immediately swung all suspicion on her.

Finally catching her breath, Diana took one step toward the festival when she saw him.

It was Detective Lucci. He moved toward her, around the people enjoying the festival, with precision and purpose . . . heading straight for the tasting room. As his foot hit the curb, he looked up and noticed her. It took him a moment to make the connection, and when he did, he raised an eyebrow in suspicion. "Signora St. James."

She waved. "Hello."

"Here for a taste of wine, eh?" His eyes danced. He seemed to delight in her discomfort. "And here I thought you wouldn't be drinking wine for a very long time."

"Well . . . I suppose I'm here for the same reason you're here. I was just browsing the festival and noticed the logo for the wine was the same as the bottle that was in Marcello's dressing room."

He raised an eyebrow. Clearly, he didn't believe that excuse one bit. "You noticed that?"

She nodded. "And of course it gave me pause. That's why you are here, is it not?"

He nodded. "And why you were standing out here, looking like you were going to be sick?"

She fanned her face. "Well . . . yes. Actually, it just struck me that I was very close to drinking that wine myself. Had he dropped dead a moment later, I might not be here."

"Very fortunate for you." He reached into his pocket and pulled out his pad. "Since you're here, I did have a few more questions for you. You said that the wine was in the dressing room when you got there, and he poured himself a glass, but not you?"

"That's right. I didn't want any, at first."

"Your fingerprints were on the bottle," he said, not looking up from his pad.

"That makes sense. They would be, because when I changed my mind, I poured my own glass."

"And two other sets. Marcello's, and—"

"Titania's," Diana finished, before she'd thought too much over whether it was wise.

"Titania?"

"Yes. I mean, Mariana Massari."

"How did you know that?" Now, he was looking even more suspicious.

"Well, I didn't know. I mean, I just guessed, because she was the last one in the dressing room before me. You see, I w—"

"Why are you here, exactly, Signora St. James?" he asked, tapping his foot. Now he seemed more annoyed than suspicious. "I want to know what would lead you to the exact spot where the bottle of wine used to murder Marcello Camillo was purchased. I hope you're not tampering with this investigation?"

She inhaled sharply. Sweat began to break out on her forehead. *I should just tell him about Titania. After all, he's going to find out the second he goes inside. But will that prove anything? She works there. That doesn't mean she's a poisoner. I'm the one who doesn't belong there, and who was in both places at the wrong time.* "Well, you see—"

"Mom!" a voice called from down the sidewalk. Suddenly, Bea was there, flinging herself into the conversation, draping an arm around Diana. "Hi, we've been looking for you. Where've you been? Did you get that bottle of wine you wanted to get for Dad?"

"Um . . ." Diana's mind went utterly blank. Wine? For Evan? Why? "Uh . . ."

"You know, for the present." Bea's eyes seemed to signal something Diana could not decipher.

"Present?" she repeated dumbly.

"You said you were going to buy that bottle of wine for him for the engagement, instead of that glass sculpture of the fat lady. I liked it

107

better, and I'm sure he'll get more use out of it. So good choice," she rambled on brightly, hugging her mother tight. She glanced at the detective, and back at Diana. "But what happened? You were gone so long, I had to come after you. Did you have trouble picking out the type? He likes reds. You always forget that. I don't know what Vidal likes, but at this point, I really don't care!"

Bea gave her a meaningful look, as if trying to transmit something telepathically. Why was she rambling on like this? Was she . . . trying to save her?

Oh.

"Yes . . ." she said, starting to catch her drift. "Right. I don't know where my mind was. Maybe you can come in and help me pick it? You know what your father likes."

Bea smiled. "I sure can. You know I love my wine. Let's get him a good Chiaretto."

Leave it to Bea to defuse the situation. Though she looked like an angel, what with her freckles and big blue eyes, she was not nearly as innocent as she let people believe. She had been known to use that to her advantage many a time, growing up, casting blame elsewhere, simply with a bat of those long eyelashes of hers. No wonder she had her daddy wrapped around her finger.

"Great. Thanks." She took Bea by the hand and started to lead her up the stairs, to the tasting room. Then she paused. "Was there anything else, Detective?"

He shook his head. "No. You go on. But just remember what I said about staying close? I might have more questions for you."

"Of course." She motioned to the wine bar. "Were you going in, too?"

He nodded. "After you."

Good, she thought. *Let him get just as suspicious at Mariana as I was. Maybe it'll keep him off my back.*

When she and Bea went inside, she scanned the area for Mariana. But she was gone. She'd likely seen the detective coming and had plenty of time to make herself scarce.

"Here, Mom, this one looks good." Bea said, thrusting a bottle into her hands.

Diana peered over at the detective, who was watching her. Ignoring him, she took the wine up to the counter. *Yes, what a perfect gift for an engagement. Possibly poisonous wine.*

As soon as she paid, she turned around to walk outside and saw Lucci talking to another worker in Italian. As he spoke, he gave her a sidelong glance.

She quickly ushered Bea to the door. She had better things to do than hang around waiting for the police to ask her more questions.

The second they went outside, though, Bea turned to her. "Okay, Mom. Level with me. What in the world is going on?"

CHAPTER EIGHTEEN

Diana hedged, looking everywhere but at her youngest daughter. She turned toward the festival. "I don't know. We should probably find Lily, don't you think she's probably starving by—"

"Mom!" Bea said, rooted to her spot on the sidewalk. "Lily's fine. She's pregnant, not dying. She can get her own food. We are not going anywhere until you tell me what's happening! It has to do with that murder of that actor, right? You're still a suspect."

Diana stared at her, wondering how much of the interaction with Detective Lucci she'd witnessed. "How did you know—"

"All right, fine," she said, rolling her eyes. "You were acting so squirrely again. I mean, that excuse—going to get an engagement gift for Vidal and Dad? Please. I saw right through it. So I left Lily at the food court and followed you. And lo and behold—"

"You *followed* me?"

She gave her a sheepish look. "I didn't want you getting into trouble."

"I can take care of my—"

"Can you? Because that police officer looked pretty close to snapping some cuffs on your wrists and hauling you downtown."

Diana finally nodded, then decided to take a page from Mariana's speech. "Oh, no he wasn't. He just had more questions. But it's not a problem, darling. I didn't do it. I have nothing to worry about."

"But why was he questioning you like that? Talk about treating you like a hostile witness."

Diana pointed at the tasting room. "I just realized the wine in the victim's dressing room came from there. I went to check it out, and obviously, the police had the same thought. They found it odd that I would be there."

"Mom . . . are you conducting an investigation on your own?" Bea's eyes widened.

"What makes you think—"

"Duh. Because you're like me. Sort of. You don't just stand by and let things happen. You have to be involved." She smiled. "Though you don't like to take many risks. Which is why I'm going to help you!"

"Oh, no you're not," Diana said, walking away.

Bea rushed to catch up to her. "Come on, Mom. I love this stuff. You know, Hai and I used to go to escape rooms all the time in Japan, and I was always MVP. I loved figuring things out. I can be your Dr. Watson!" She clapped her hands.

"This is not an escape room, darling. This is my life. And we're not figuring anything out."

She pouted. "Mom. You're no fun. Come on. Tell me more about the case. So what? When you went into this actor's dressing room, the wine was already there?"

Diana nodded. Actually, it would be nice to talk this out with someone who was on her side. "Yes, it was. And Mariana Massari, the woman who played Titania, brought it to him. She works at the tasting room," she explained. "That was what I was doing in there—talking to her. It turns out she had a big crush on him, which was not reciprocated."

"Ah. She sounds like the obvious suspect. So why aren't the police going after her?"

Diana shrugged. "She sounds good, I agree. But the thing is, I don't believe she did it. She was really torn up about his death."

"Hello? She's an actress."

"But it's more than that. I mean, if you wanted to kill someone and worked for a winery that your family owned, it'd be pretty stupid to poison the wine. That's like putting a target right on your forehead."

"Her family owns the winery? Huh." She thought for a moment. "Or *maybe* that was what she was *thinking* people would think. She knew they'd discount her, because she'd be *too* obvious a suspect."

Diana stopped and turned to her. "Where did you get such a devious mind? It wasn't from me, and it's certainly not from your father." Evan was book-smart, but he lacked all common sense.

"I read a lot of Agatha Christie," she explained with a shrug. "The library at the school in Japan doesn't have a lot of books in English. Mostly just Hercule Poirot books. I can pretty much tell you the murderer in every one of them. This sounds a lot like *The Mysterious Affair at Styles*."

"It does?"

She nodded. "Yes, when this rich old lady died of poisoning, at first, everyone thought the gold-digging husband was to blame. It was obvious. He didn't do anything to hide his guilt, either. But then they arrested him and tried him, which was just what he wanted, because he couldn't be tried for the same crime twice. Then—"

"Mariana *is* trying to hide it. And believe me, she doesn't want to be arrested for it. She says she doesn't want the scandal to mess with her acting career."

"She is? Oh. Hmm," Bea said, tapping her chin. "So who else could've poisoned the bottle?"

"Really, anyone who was backstage. So that's any one of fifty people. Mariana showed me a way that you could pop a cork with a lighter, put poison in, and then close it up, so anyone could've done it, as long as they were back there."

"Are you sure it was in the bottle? In *The Mysterious Affair at Styles,* they all thought it was in the coffee, but it turned out to be in her—"

"He was drinking the wine when he died, so they assume it was."

"But maybe it wasn't. Maybe it was something entirely different nobody was thinking about!" she remarked, to Diana's surprise. She'd certainly raised a skeptical child. She knew Bea was one to question everything, but she hadn't realized how good she was at it.

"Well, no one will know until after the autopsy, and I'm sure the police won't be sharing the details with me."

She nodded. "Right. I think there's only one thing to do."

"Which is . . .?"

"Go back to the scene of the crime."

Diana shook her head. Yes, the thought had occurred to her, but she'd just got done telling herself there was no way she could go back there. "Impossible."

"Why impossible?"

"Because I tried to go back this morning. If the director sees me, he'll sic the police on me. He thinks for sure I'm the murderer, because I was with Marcello when he died."

She rubbed her hands together deviously and grinned. "Well, that's why you have me."

"No, I don't. Like I said, you're not—"

Suddenly, the phone in Bea's hands buzzed. She looked at it. "That's Lily. She's pissed I ditched her at the food court and now she's enduring Vidal and Dad making out in front of her. They're at some café on the other side of the piazza now. We probably have to go and check on them before they get too suspicious."

Diana decided that was a much better idea than dragging her youngest into this mess she'd found herself in. "You're on. Let's go."

"Good," she said, linking arms with her mother. "On the way we can think of a good excuse to ditch them so you and I can go backstage at the theater and check things out, Sherlock."

"Wait. What? Absolutely not!"

Diana glared at Bea, who looked straight ahead, smiling that innocent smile of hers that made everyone think she could do no wrong.

*

Diana and her daughter made it to a café just outside the festival for a late lunch. She was happy to see that they'd selected a table outdoors, under a yellow umbrella. Though she already knew from experience that she wouldn't enjoy the company of Evan and Tilda, at least she could enjoy the warm weather.

"I don't think this is a good idea," she muttered to her youngest as they approached. "Maybe we just enjoy lunch and—"

"Mom. Trust me. We've got this."

Diana sighed. Her daughter never had been one to take no for an answer. And maybe she was right. Maybe she did need Bea's help.

Evan stood up as they approached. He was wearing the awful hat, a purple velvet creation with a massive peacock feather, cocked on his head. It was capturing quite a bit of attention from those around them, who seemed to be looking at him with expressions that said, *Idiot American.* Diana wasn't in much of a humorous mood, but she found herself stifling a laugh behind her hand.

"Great hat, Dad," Bea muttered, in a way that Diana interpreted to mean, *I really don't want to be seen with you.*

"Ladies," he said, as Diana thrust the bottle of Chiaretto into his hands.

"For you," she said with a smile. "For your engagement. Bea told me you'd like it."

He smiled down at it. "How thoughtful of you, love. But you didn't have to."

113

Tilda grabbed it, dipped her sunglasses, and looked at the label, her pert nose wrinkling. "I like white Zinfandel."

That's why I didn't buy it, Diana thought, but Bea filled in before she could retort. "It's a pale red. You'll both like it."

"This isn't poisoned, is it?" Tilda asked with a sweet smile.

Evan elbowed her.

"What?" she asked innocently. "You can't pretend Diana doesn't have a *little* bit of a history with poisoned wine."

Diana reached across. "Fine. I could take it back."

"No, no," Evan said, clearly eager to defuse the situation. "It's a lovely gift, Diana. And so appreciated."

They sat down together. "So what have you found in the festival?" Diana asked them, slipping a napkin over her lap and looking down at her sore foot. She slipped the shoe off discreetly. Sure enough, she now had two little blisters on the side of her foot. She repositioned her sock. "Anything good?"

She leaned forward and listened as Evan went off on some street show they'd watched, with all the players on stilts. "It had a very Cirque du Soleil vibe to it. You'd have liked it, Di."

Diana smiled. He remembered how much she loved Cirque du Soleil when they'd seen a show before.

"Well, I didn't like it. It was totally creepy," Tilda said, swirling her wine in her glass. She was wearing a low-cut pink top that exposed most of her cleavage, and shorts so small, they looked practically illegal. From the way she slurred that sentence, Diana had the inkling she was already drunk. After one glass? What had she missed? "I hate clowns."

"I thought you liked the music, sweetie?" Evan said, taking her hand and patting it.

"No. And what was with that guy in the floppy hat and tights? Any guy who wears tights is a little screwed up in the head," she muttered, staring into her wine glass.

"You mean . . . Shakespeare?" Lily asked.

Bea snorted. "Imagine that. Someone dressed as Shakespeare at a Shakespeare festival. What will they think of next?"

Diana elbowed her as they looked over the menus. It was all a show, really, because she and Bea had made other plans. But oh, the *Risotto all'Amarone* looked absolutely delicious. And traipsing around Verona had given her an appetite. Too bad.

"Oh, I'm feeling a little faint," Bea said suddenly, fanning her face.

That was Diana's cue. Before she could open her mouth, Evan slid a water glass over to her. "It's hot. Drink."

She took a sip of water and then clutched her stomach. "Oh, oh no. I feel terrible."

"You look green," Tilda remarked, not looking up from her menu.

Lily leaned forward. "No she doesn't. But she does look flushed." She put a hand on her forehead. "Hot. It could be sunstroke?"

"Do you want me to take you back to the house?" Diana offered.

"Yes, that would probably be best," Bea said, maybe a little too readily, her chair scraping on the brick patio as she pushed away from the table. Even so, she was a formidable actress.

As Diana lifted her purse and prepared to leave, too, Evan closed his menu. "We'll all go. We can get something at the villa. Gaia said—"

Diana held up a hand. "Not necessary. Really."

Bea's voice was weak, hovering on death's door. "Yeah, Daddy. I don't want to spoil your meal."

He started to shake his head, but Tilda grabbed his arm and spoke up first. "Yes, Evan. Let's not spoil this. It's so nice here and I am so hungry. I want to get a Stromboli and eat until I throw up and I look as pregnant and bloated as Lily." She puffed her taut stomach out and patted it.

Lily scowled and gave Diana a glance that said, *Please don't leave me here alone with them.*

Evan gave her a doubtful look, and then looked back at Diana. "How will you get home? It's pretty far."

Bea, still grimacing in mock-pain, held up her phone. "I've got GPS. We'll handle it." She doubled over and let out a groan. "Now, Mommy. Let's go. I'm dying."

Okay, Bea, maybe let's not overdo this? Diana thought as she put an arm around her youngest. Bea leaned into her, now clasping both hands over her stomach, as if she was getting ready to birth an alien. "We'd better go. Enjoy the festival. See you back at the house!" she said, leading her away.

"Ohhh. Ohhhhhh," Bea moaned as they staggered toward the curb. Nearby diners turned to look at her.

"Bea, you can cut the hysterics," Diana mumbled when they'd turned a corner.

Bea straightened and smiled. "Good. Let's go to the theater, Mommy."

CHAPTER NINETEEN

Diana was expecting the theater to be swarming with people getting ready for the three o'clock show, but when they arrived, the place was deserted. There was a sign on the front saying that the show had been cancelled due to "unforeseen circumstances," likely because the police hadn't yet given them the all-clear.

Bea marched to the front of the theater, as Diana straggled behind, hoping the director wasn't anywhere nearby. She tried the door. "Locked."

Diana nodded, still hiding behind her daughter. "It was before. There's a door on the side."

"Oh? Let's go." Bea started to break into a run, but stopped when Diana didn't follow. "What?"

She sighed. "I'm kind of on the director's bad side. If he sees me here, it'll be off with my head."

Bea grinned. "Oh, Mommy. You're such a goody-goody. Come on. Live a little. Take a walk on the wild side with me, okay?"

Diana could've told her that she *had* lived. She could've told her that in Paris, she'd climbed a building and sneaked into a possible murderer's bedroom to find a necklace. But not only had she nearly gotten herself thrown in jail . . . she'd also almost had a heart attack. She really wasn't sure she wanted to relive that stress.

But she knew her daughter. If she said no, Bea would strike out and try to get answers on her own. She couldn't let Bea risk getting in trouble. So the only thing she could do was go along with her.

"All right. I'm coming," she muttered, following her, head down. "But slowly. My shoe's been giving me blisters. I think one just burst."

They stopped for a second so Diana could adjust her shoe. Though it'd been a sensible walking shoe, something was amiss, because one of the blisters on the side of her foot had indeed burst.

"Ow, that looks painful," Bea said, looking around impatiently.

Diana fixed her sock. "I'll manage."

They walked, Diana limping slightly, around the curve of the arena, to the back door. It was closed this time. When they got there, Bea stopped, her hand on the door handle. "Was there anyone in here the last time?"

"A janitor. And the director came back later." She shuddered at the memory of him shooing her from the theater.

She paused with her ear to the door, listening. "I don't hear anything."

"Maybe there's no one in there."

Bea tugged on the door. It opened. Bea smiled in delight. Diana frowned. She was almost hoping it *wouldn't* open, so she could go back to the villa and calm her nerves with a big glass of wine. Where had her daughter gotten such pluck, such bravery?

Definitely *not* from her, that was for sure.

"First rule in being a spy: Open doors with caution." Bea peered in and smiled. She whispered, "I don't see anyone!"

Diana gritted her teeth. How could her daughter treat this like some joke? They would be in some major trouble if they got caught. But that was Bea. She had her charm and cuteness, which got her out of the stickiest situations. Diana didn't have that luxury. Her stomach dropped like a cannonball in her gut as Bea slipped inside.

Diana followed into the dark back room. When she let the door close behind them, slowly as to make only the smallest of noises, it left them in almost pitch blackness. They stumbled over each other, until Bea found her hand and squeezed it tight. "No problem. Easy-peasy," she said as Diana's eyes adjusted.

There was a light up ahead. Two of them, actually. A dull blue was coming from the direction of the stage. Another appeared to be coming from the hallway that contained the dressing rooms. Diana pointed. "I think we just need to go—"

A voice shouted suddenly in Italian, and then there were footsteps coming toward them.

Diana's heart stopped. Her eyes, wide, found Bea's, who looked just as shocked. Without a word, they broke apart and rushed for hiding spots. Diana slid behind a giant spotlight, Bea behind a clothing rack. Peering from behind it, Diana saw a couple of actors, rushing on stage.

More Italian. Then someone began to speak. She recognized it as the second scene of the first act, the introduction of Quince, the carpenter, who is trying to put on a play with the other tradesmen.

So they were rehearsing the play. That meant that Pietro, the director, was likely nearby. *Nope. I'm done with this,* Diana thought, looking for the door. *This is stupid and insane.*

In the darkness, she could just make out Bea's face behind the clothing rack. *Let's get out of here,* she mouthed.

Bea crawled from her hiding place and whispered, "Are you kidding? This is perfect. They're all on stage, rehearsing. So all I need to do is go to his dressing room. Which one is it?"

Diana shook his head. "You don't know what you're looking for. I should do it."

"You would?" Now it was Bea's turn to look doubtful.

Truthfully, she wasn't sure. Maybe. She could do that. From the front lobby, Marcello's dressing room was at the end of the hall, closest to the stage, so it was the last one she'd come to, last night. Coming this way, from the back, it would likely be the first one she'd arrive at. She'd only be in danger a few seconds, at the most.

She sat there as the players went through their lines on stage, taking deep breath after deep breath, trying to psych herself up. Then she took a big gulp of air and let it out slowly. "I can do this."

Bea smiled. "I know you can." She looked down and picked something up. "You should wear this."

"What is it?"

"I don't know. I found it over there, by the stairs. A disguise."

Diana turned it over in her head before she realized just what it was. It was the huge donkey's head that Nick Bottom wore when Puck changes him into an ass. She stared at it, thinking that yes, she was an ass, for ever thinking this was a good idea.

Then she slipped it over her head. It smelled a little like cigarettes, a little like morning breath, and the eye slits made it near-impossible to see out of. Also, how did people *breathe*, much less speak lines, in these things? Diana suspected she'd be having trouble breathing, even without the mask. But it also sort of insulated her from the outside world, like a suit of armor.

She rose to her feet and whispered, more to herself than to Bea, "I can do this."

"Yes you can. I'll stay here and if anyone comes by, I'll try to stall them. Okay?"

"Okay," Diana mumbled, nodding her massive donkey head, and stumbled off toward the staircase, hands in front of her, since she couldn't really see where her feet were going. The donkey head was so giant, its ear scraped against the rack of costumes before getting caught on a hanger. She felt the thing start to lift off her head before reaching back and freeing herself, then continuing on.

She hit the first step with the toes of her shoes and flailed her hand to the right, looking for a handrail or wall to hold onto. The blister on her foot screamed in protest. With the metal of the railing firmly in her hand, she quickly scaled the steps. Grabbing the doorknob to Marcello's room like a lifeline, she turned it, pushed the door open, and slipped inside, trying not to get tangled in the crime-scene tape.

The room was dark. When she was inside, she ripped off the mask, static crackling in her hair, and drew in an uneasy breath. She scanned the area, hardly knowing where to look first. Much had been removed from the room, probably by the police. The wine bottle was not there, but the tray that it and the glasses had sat upon was sitting atop the dresser, empty. No, if she was going to find any interesting clue to the identity of the murderer, it'd likely be hidden.

The white linen shirt Marcello had been changing out of was draped over the top of the screen. She touched it, leaning into it. It even still smelled like the cigarette he'd been smoking, shortly before his death. It almost looked as if he'd just stepped out for a minute, as if he was one of the actors, on stage, rehearsing right now.

Her eyes caught on the spot behind the screen, where she'd first seen Marcello's lifeless body. Heat flooded her face, and her heart began to palpitate erratically.

Concentrate, Diana.

Taking a step forward, she dove for couch. She got to her knees and peered underneath, finding nothing but a discarded shoe. Shuffling to the side of it, she found a trunk with drawers. She opened them, one by one, finding nothing but stage makeup and costume accessories.

Still on her knees, she pivoted, her lips twisting. *Think, Diana. Think.*

The dresser. Of course. She crossed over to it and began to open those drawers, as well. Stationery. Cards from admirers that had probably once accompanied lovely bouquets. She read one of them. *I burn for you, my love – G.*

Hmm. Well, she'd always known he was a womanizer, even before Luca told her that, because as good-looking as he was, how could he not be? But as she went through the cards, finding similar messages, her stomach churned. He wasn't just a womanizer. He was a serial collector of women's affections. He probably had a clan of women groupies in numbers that rivaled the population of some small countries.

She sat back on her haunches, thinking. He'd encouraged the affection of so many women, but . . . Mariana, he'd shoved off. Often. That was strange, wasn't it?

Maybe he really did care for her, but didn't want to admit it and blow his reputation. Sad.

She shoved a drawer closed and opened another one. Nothing. Everything that could've been construed as evidence had clearly already been removed by the police.

Still on her knees, she reached under the dresser, sweeping her hand along the thick carpet. Her fingers touched paper.

Falling to her stomach and shuffling closer to the dresser, she reached as far as her fingers could, grabbed an edge of the paper, and dragged it forward. When she brought it to light, she recognized the shape instantly. It was another piece of origami, folded into a rose.

But on this one, instead of her name, it said, *Linda.*

Who was Linda? And why would he still be holding onto that note? Did he do that at every show, pick out a woman to woo and lure to his dressing room? The man at the door hadn't seemed to think so, but he was old. Or maybe he was just trying to spare her feelings.

Still, when had he intended to give this note to Linda? *Diana* was at his last performance. Maybe she was one of the smart ones who had decided not to show up, at an earlier performance. But no . . . Diana had been at opening night. So who was this woman?

Slipping it open, she read:

Lovely Linda,

You look so beautiful out there. Please meet me backstage after the show. I'll be waiting for you.

Yours,

M.

So basically, word for word, the same message she'd received.

But why was this letter here? Had he handed out notes to more than one woman for opening night, hoping one of them would dare to meet him backstage? Had this lady realized what a womanizer he was and left this as his calling card? After all, if the note had gotten Diana backstage, it had likely gotten others backstage, too.

121

Nothing made sense.

She looked around some more, feeling helpless. The photographs of Marcello, with various movie starlets on his arm, stared down at her, seeming to say, *You must find who did this. You're missing something.*

But the more she looked, the less convinced she became that whatever she was looking for was here. There was nothing else.

Taking a deep breath, she turned toward the door and slipped the donkey mask over her head. It was only when she yanked the door toward her that she heard the voices in the corridor.

The voices suddenly went quiet, and she cringed. She'd been spotted.

What had Bea *just* said to her? *First rule in being a spy: Open doors with caution.*

Probably the first of many reasons why she'd never applied for a stint in the CIA.

CHAPTER TWENTY

No going back now, Diana thought, her hand clammy on the doorknob. *Whoever is out there knows you're here.*

At that moment, she felt very much like the animal whose head she was wearing.

She poked her head out totally, to find a man she recognized as Oberon, king of the fairies, from the play. She was sure of it—he had a pointed, trimmed beard and was short in stature. But for some reason, he wasn't wearing the wings and tights of the fairies. He was wearing a hat similar to one that Lysander wore. He was walking toward her, frowning.

Her vision blurred. It felt mighty stuffy within the confines of the mask, as if it was squeezing her cranium. *Oh god, here it comes . . .*

He stopped in front of her. "Roberto!" he shouted, then started to go on in mile-a-minute Italian. Diana simply nodded her ass-head and took it, unsure of what he was saying. He motioned grandly with his hands, then beckoned for her to follow him.

Her heart stopped as she realized where he was asking her to go.

He wanted her on the stage.

She started shaking her donkey-head, now, fervently. There was no way she'd go on the stage. But she couldn't get away. She glanced toward the end of the hallway, to the door to outside, to freedom, and saw Bea peeking out from behind a rack of clothes, finally looking as truly horrified and scared as Diana had felt, *this entire time.*

She mouthed, *Help me,* but then she realized she was being stupid—Bea couldn't see her mouth. She was wearing a donkey-head.

Meanwhile, Oberon continued to shout to *Stefano,* who must be the actor that had been chosen to play Quince after Marcello's death. Something about how the scene was going on and they'd been looking for him, she thought. Oberon actually got behind Diana and began to nudge her toward the stage, as if she really was some obstinate ass that needed the extra shove in the behind.

She let out a little moan. She'd never felt more like an ass than she did right then. This was absolutely ridiculous. She might as well give herself up right now.

As she reached for her mask, ready to rip it off her head, suddenly, out of nowhere, someone shouted, *"Fuoco!"*

Fuoco? It sounded like a dirty word. Diana was momentarily confused until the same voice, Bea's voice, screamed, "Fire!" Suddenly, an alarm began to clang overhead.

Oberon's eyes filled with dread. He turned and bolted down the hallway, toward his dressing room, mumbling something in Italian. Doors on either side of the hallway opened, and the halls filled with actors, all heading for the front doors. Diana slinked down the back stairs, toward the exit. She threw off her donkey mask, tossed it aside, and rushed outside. Bea was leaning against the wall of the adjacent building.

"Find anything?"

Diana was so breathless, she could hardly speak. The blood was still rushing through her ears. Smoothing her flyaway hair down around the crown of her head, she began to power-walk toward the sidewalk. She wanted to get as far away from this theater as possible, so she reached back, took Bea's hand and rushed her out to the main street.

When she got there, away from the commotion, she said, still hyped up on the adrenaline, "That was terrifying."

Bea laughed. "Oh, Mom, you need to get out more. It wasn't even a little scary. You were in no danger whatsoever among those *scary* actors."

Diana glared at her daughter, wondering exactly what danger she'd been getting into in Japan, if that little episode was so mild to her. "*You* weren't in danger, Miss Hide-Behind-the-Costume-Rack. I was. *I* almost had to go out on stage and act out the part of Nick Bottom—in Italian!"

She giggled. "I think that might've actually made me want to see *A Midsummer Night's Dream*, for once in my life. It would've been hilarious."

"For you, maybe." She shuddered, but even she had to admit it was kind of funny. She started to laugh, too. "Seriously, though! I wouldn't be alive, if I did go out on the stage. The director hates me. He'd have probably had me arrested, but not before I passed out from pure humiliation."

"Oh, shush," Bea said, waving that idea away. "I took care of things. My shouting Fire at the opportune moment saved the day, didn't it?" She blew on her fingernails and pretended to buff them on her T-shirt. "I told you I had your back, Mom."

"Hmm," Diana said. "You sure are a superhero!"

The theater was no longer in sight, so Diana slowed her pace. By now, her blister was screaming on her foot. Bea stopped altogether, so Diana loosened her shoe to take a look. It was redder than before. She needed a Band-Aid.

Bea said, "So? Tell me everything! Did you find a smoking gun?"

"Not even close. I found nothing."

Bea's nose wrinkled. "Come on. That was the scene of the crime. You had to have found *something*."

Diana shook her head. "The scene of the crime was combed over by every police officer in this town, I'm sure. There was nothing even remotely interesting there, unless you count a note that he sent a woman, similar to the one he sent me."

Bea's jaw dropped. "He sent you a love note? Really? That's awesome! When?"

"It wasn't a love note. It was a folded thing, just asking for me to visit him backstage after the performance. That's all."

"Oh!" She clutched at her heart. "That's so romantic."

Diana rolled her eyes. "Bea, it's not really all that romantic considering that one, it's looking like he sent letters to quite a few women, and two, he's dead. So really, pardon me for not being flattered."

"Oh, Mom," she said, her voice laced with pity, as something must've just occurred to her. "But you went backstage to meet him, so were you thinking . . .?" She patted her heart again. "Oh, Mommy."

She shook her head and took Bea's hand. Heartbreak as a twenty-year-old was a life-ending thing. But Diana had met with enough disappointment in life to know not to hitch her hopes to some actor. Still, she had had those silly thoughts of falling in love, of happily-ever-after. And no, while it wasn't life-ending, it was just sad.

"It's fine, love. I'm not upset. In fact, I'm glad," she said with a smile. "After all, if I had met the man of my dreams here, I would have less time to spend with you."

Bea reached over and hugged her mom. "Yes. Men. Who needs them?" she muttered, but even as she did, her expression turned stormy.

"Hai hasn't called?"

She shook her head. "I think it might be over between us."

Diana wrapped an arm around her. She had a flashback to when Bea would skin her knee during one of her many outdoor adventures, and come in crying, wanting mommy to make it all better. Back then, an ice pack and an ice cream had always done the trick.

"Well, Dr. Watson, what do you say I treat you to a gelato?" she asked.

Bea smiled. "I'd love that. Thanks, Mom. I'm starving."

They started to walk down the street, as Bea thumbed in directions, trying to find the location of the nearest gelato shop.

Suddenly, she looked up. "Wait. You said there was a love letter for someone else there. In *Peril at End House*, that was the key to solving the whole mystery."

"Maybe but real life isn't anything like an Agatha Christie mystery, where it's obvious which of millions of potential clues you can discount, and which ones actually mean something. It's far more confusing than that."

"Okay, true. But was there any name on the letter? Who was it for?"

"Someone named Linda," Diana said. "But I don't know how we'd find—"

She stopped and stood still in the street. Of course.

"Scratch that. I'll have to get you that gelato later. I have an idea that Watson and Holmes need to investigate. Now."

Bea laughed. "As much as I love gelato, I'd much rather be your Watson!"

*

The women raced up the street, back toward the festival. By then, the crowds were worse than before, so they had to weave their way among festival-goers on the busy sidewalk.

"Come on. I have an idea," Diana said, leading Bea outside and up the street and down the alley. When she approached her door, she was just about to ring the doorbell when the door swung open.

Mariana stood there, her shock soon morphing to annoyance. "What are you doing here?"

126

"We have questions for you," Diana said, barring her way on the front stoop.

She pulled her purse up on her shoulder and shook her head. "I'm sorry. I don't have time for this. They're practicing Act Two at the theater, and I'm already late."

Bea smiled. "Oh, you don't have to worry about that. There's been a little delay in the rehearsal." She winked at Diana.

Mariana studied her. "How do you know? And for that matter, who *are* you?"

"She's my daughter," Diana explained. "We just came from the theater. And—"

"You have? Did you speak to Pietro? I doubt they're even going to let us have a show. They delayed it until tonight, but I'm thinking they're going to cancel it since the police don't seem to know anything about who did this horrible thing." She sighed.

"It might help if you told them what you know," Diana muttered.

She sighed. "I told you, I can't. Are we done here?" She tried to push past them.

Diana moved aside, but Bea stood firm, crossing her arms. "Wait. Who's Linda?"

Mariana stopped. Her eyes widened a bit with recognition. "Linda?"

Diana pulled the letter out of her pocket and handed it to the actress. "I found this in his dressing room."

She stared at it, then up at Diana. "Wait. . . what were you doing in his dressing room?"

"That's not important," Diana said, blushing at the thought of herself traipsing around in that donkey mask. "Do you know who this person is, or not?"

"Of course not. You think I kept track of all of Marcello's women?" she said, avoiding her gaze. "Now if you'll excuse me, I—"

"You loved Marcello. You told me that. I think you know more about Marcello's women than you're letting on," Diana stated.

She started to shake her head, and then she sighed. "Linda. Yes, I suppose she was one of our troupe groupies."

"Troupe groupies?" Bea asked.

"Yes. We have several. Most of them are in love with Marcello."

Bea said, "The note is in English. Is she—"

"Yes, I believe she's American, living in town. I don't know where she lives, but I know where she works. The Caffè Al Teatro."

That struck a chord. Diana had been there. "Wait . . . doesn't Luca Castille live over there?"

She shrugged. "Luca? Maybe. I don't know."

"I was in that café. I talked to an American barista this morning. She told me she was a big fan of Marcello's."

"And?" Bea asked. "Was she acting weird?"

Diana frowned, trying to remember if she'd been acting oddly at all. No, she hadn't. In fact, from the way she spoke, she didn't sound like she even knew Marcello was dead. She shook her head.

Still . . . it was a lead. The best one she had.

"Thanks, Mariana." She took her daughter by the arm. "Come on, Watson. Let's go ask Linda some questions."

CHAPTER TWENTY ONE

When Diana and Bea arrived, Caffè Al Teatro was buzzing. It seemed to be filled with well-dressed people who'd come to see the performance, only to find out that it had been delayed. As Diana and Bea stood in the long line, stretching nearly out the door, Bea stood on her tiptoes.

"Is that the lady?" Bea asked, pointing toward the front of the room.

Diana tried to stand on the tips of her own toes, but it did no good. She was several inches shorter than her daughter, even without the funny platform sneakers her daughter was fond of wearing. She tried to move to the side, but there was a wall in the way. "I don't know. What does she look like?"

"Kind of overweight. Middle-aged. Glasses. Oh, and the bottom of her hair is blue."

Diana nodded. "That's her."

"Good. She's still working here." Bea reached into her wristlet. "I'm getting the biggest, baddest thing for me possible. It's been hours since I was cheated out of my pizza, my lunch, my gelato . . ."

Diana laughed. "Hey, you volunteered for this. Nobody said being a detective was easy."

Finally, they approached the counter. Luckily, it was Linda who waited on them. She looked at Diana through slightly bleary red eyes. "Hey, New York. I remember you! Couldn't get enough of us, could you? What can I get you?"

Bea leaned over the counter like a traveler at an oasis who hadn't had a drink in days. "Espresso. And . . ." She looked at the display case and pointed out her selections. "One of those chocolate things . . . one of those little strawberry ones . . . and one of those cream-puff things with the powdered sugar."

Diana looked over at her poor, starving Watson. Leave it to Bea to complete forget about their mission when it came to satisfying her sweet tooth. Linda nodded and looked at Diana. "And for you?"

"Nothing. Thank you. I was wondering--"

The barista held up a finger and turned to get the espresso. As she did, Diana laid the origami flower on the counter.

When the barista turned around, she caught sight of it and tilted her head. "What's that?" She smiled. "And why does it have my name on it?"

"We were hoping that you could tell us, Linda?" Diana said. "It came from Marcello Camillo's dressing room at the theater. I believe he may have planned to give it to you?"

Linda stared at it, her smiled disappearing. Then her face crinkled, and she began to cry. She looked around helplessly, then plucked a few napkins from the dispenser. "Oh, it's terrible," she sniffled. "I heard what happened to him. Everyone's been talking about it. Excuse me . . ."

She pulled away from the counter, whispered something to one of the baristas, and rushed into the back room.

Bea laid her hand on the display case, stared forlornly at her pastry, and let out a big sigh. "So close, and yet so far away."

Ignoring her, Diana watched the door the woman had passed through. "Come on, Bea."

She marched behind the counter and through the door to the back room. The woman, sitting on a stool and dotting her eyes with a handkerchief, straightened in surprise. "I'm sorry," she said, wiping her eyes. "I just get so emotional. I really can't believe he's gone. He was such a great talent. I've been following the troupe for some time, you see, and—"

"So you saw him in *A Midsummer Night's Dream?*"

She shook her head. "I saw him in other plays, though. He's so good. So handsome. You see, I was in the theater program myself, in Jersey, so I love all things theater and Shakespeare."

"You were there yesterday?"

"Oh, no. You can ask my boss. I was here, at work, the entire time. But I was going to go to today's performance. I was invited."

"Today's?"

She nodded. "And it just so happened I came by a ticket for today's performance. I couldn't wait to see him play Oberon, but when it was cancelled, I decided to pick up an extra—"

"Oberon?" Diana asked. "Marcello played Quince."

She frowned. "No. I'm sure I heard that he was playing Oberon . . ."

130

Diana reached into her bag and pulled out the program. She opened to the picture of Marcello. "Is this the man who you thought played Oberon?"

She shook her head. "No . . . who is he?" She read the name. "Wait. That's Marcello? The one who died?"

Diana flipped to the picture of the man who played Oberon, the one who'd accosted her while she was wearing the donkey head. His name was Alfonzo Rivalta. "This man?"

"Oh, yes. That's him . . . ." Her jaw dropped. "Are you saying that he's not dead?"

Bea nodded. "That's exactly what she's saying. We just saw him. He's alive and kicking and at the theater right now."

Diana didn't want to be reminded of that. "Why were you confused?"

"I don't know, honestly." She picked the program up and flipped to the picture of Marcello. "So *this* is the man who died? You're sure?"

Diana nodded.

"I don't understand. He was the one who came to the café yesterday, while I was working. He gave me a ticket for today's performance. I thought it was odd, but I couldn't deny I was thrilled. I didn't even know him to pass the time of day. I thought that maybe he did it because I was such a good patron of the theater. That's all." She looked at the flower in Diana's hand. "And he meant to give me that rose? I don't know why. I've barely talked to him. I mean, he hung around here a couple of times. Flirted with me. But it never went anywhere, because I was interested in Oberon. And he flirted with all the girls. Obviously, I didn't even know that man was the real Marcello." She patted her chest. "I am so glad my Oberon is still alive. That is a relief, I tell you."

"Thank you," Diana said, turning to leave.

But Marcello is still dead. And no one seems to know who did it. Or, now, if he was even the intended victim.

*

As they went outside, Bea groaned. "So much for my food."

Diana blinked. "You can go in and get something. I didn't mean to—"

"Forget it. The line's too long now. And this is so confusing. I don't think well on an empty stomach. I'm telling you . . . if my stomach was full, the murderer would've already been caught by now."

Diana churned her conversation with Linda over in her head. "I'm sorry. We can go back to the villa if you want? Get something there?"

Bea nodded, so they began to walk that way. "Let me text Lily to tell her we'll meet her there."

She stopped to thumb in the note and winced. "So Lily's sent me about four hundred texts. She tells me that she has disowned us for leaving her in the company of Vidal." She giggled. "Vidal bought that fat lady sculpture."

Diana snorted. "Seriously?"

Bea laughed. "I guess Lily convinced her it'd look nice on the mantel in their living room."

"Well, at least they'll have a souvenir to remember the trip by," Diana said, not really paying attention.

Bea said something else, but Diana didn't hear.

"What?"

"I was just saying that Lily wants us back at the villa right away. She's there and wondering why we're not, because I was so sick at the restaurant."

"Oh," Diana murmured, still thinking of Linda. The poor woman had clearly been confused. Marcello was a known womanizer. Wanted to collect women. Had he been jealous of Linda's adoration of Alfonzo, and wanted to sway her affections toward him?

"Mom? Hello? Earth to Mom?"

Diana snapped from her thoughts. "Sorry, hon. I'm trying to understand why Linda was so confused. As a groupie, you'd think she would know all the actors. Right?"

"Not necessarily. It kind of reminds me of *Thirteen at Dinner*. They all thought someone disguised as Lady Edgeware had killed her husband, but the fact was that Lady Edgeware hired an impersonator to pretend to be her at the dinner party, so that *she* could go and kill her husband herself. She was an actress, too. The murderer *wanted* everyone to be confused."

Diana squeezed her eyes closed with confusion. Her shoulders slumped. It felt like all the pieces were there, but something was missing, and Bea wasn't helping by adding more information instead of sifting through what they already had. "What does that have to do with anything?"

"Well, they realized that it was the other way around from what they were all thinking. Linda thought that Marcello was Oberon, when actually *Alfonzo* was Oberon. So maybe the poison was intended for Alfonzo. What I don't get is how she got it in her head that Marcello was Oberon."

"Well, it makes sense. In a troupe, I think they're used to switching roles often. That's probably why Oberon was wearing a different costume in the hallway, earlier . . . because they're so very used to switching everything up like that . . ."

"But why did Marcello stop by with a ticket for Linda? Why did he write out that letter, then, if he knew that she wasn't interested in him?"

"I don't know. He was interested in her, obviously. He flirted with her. So maybe he just wanted to impress her. And somehow, she got it in her head that Marcello was playing Oberon."

Diana blinked.

Of course. "Wait . . . I have an idea. What if he was playing Oberon?"

"You said he was playing Quince."

"For the show yesterday. But . . ." She stopped and clapped her hands together. "Bea, text Lily and tell her we can't meet her at home just yet. We're too close now. And I think I know who the killer is."

133

CHAPTER TWENTY TWO

This time, as they ran, Diana was in the lead, so breathless and exhilarated, she couldn't stop if she wanted to. Blister be damned; it hardly hurt at all, now.

It all made sense. Finally, everything made sense.

"Mom!" Bea called from behind her, seemingly farther and farther away. "Mommy! Slow down!"

Diana couldn't. She didn't stop until the theater came into view. When it did, she tried to rush across the street, only to nearly be flattened by a tiny Fiat, which honked at her. Bea pulled her back just in time.

"Hey, Mom?" Bea said as she stood there, breathing hard, her lungs burning. "Let's try not to have another death on our hands?"

Diana nodded, and this time, looked both ways. "Sorry. Where did that car come from?"

"I told you to live a little, take a walk on the wild side, but that didn't mean getting yourself killed," she said. "There's a difference between reckless and downright suicidal."

Bea was right, and Diana was glad to hear such words of wisdom coming from her daughter. Maybe Bea hadn't been getting into as much trouble in Japan as Diana had feared. "You're right. We'll be careful."

Linking arms, they walked across the street to the front doors. This time, they were open. When Diana pulled one open, her heart still beating like mad, Bea said, "Wait. Didn't you say you'd get killed if you showed your face here again?"

Diana shrugged. "It's a chance I'll have to take. This is important, Bea."

"Trust me. The only way this is a good idea is if you know who the killer is and are ready to make a big reveal. Otherwise, you can wind up in a lot of trouble, throwing accusations around without —"

She stopped when she saw the look Diana was giving her.

"Wait . . . *do* you know who it is?" Bea asked. "Like, seriously? So, who?"

Diana didn't answer, so busy was she rushing inside, toward the box office.

Bea stayed on her heels. "Mom! Tell me!"

Bea's cries of exasperation were soon drowned out by the sound of actors, on stage, reciting the lines from *A Midsummer Night's Dream*. Their voices echoed around the stone arena. Diana made it to the back of the theater in time to see the mostly empty theater. The stage was full of actors, most notably Mariana Massari, as Titania, fawning over Nick Bottom, who was wearing the head of the donkey Diana had recently gotten close to. Diana didn't know the exact words, but she imagined them in English: *On the first view to say, to swear, I love thee.*

She took a deep breath. *No time to waste. You can do this.*

Diana took the steps toward the stage as quickly as she could, trying not to stumble on the old, crumbling stone. As she made her way closer, the few people in the aisles watching the rehearsal began to turn toward her.

"Mom, I hope you know what you're doing," Bea mumbled, following behind her.

"*Signora!*" someone called to her in a whisper. She couldn't understand what else they said, but she caught the drift: *This is a closed rehearsal. You are not allowed here.*

Before she knew it, men were rushing down the aisles on either side of her, trying to intercept her. Mariana, on stage, stopped speaking and squinted into the audience, shielding her eyes from the glow of the spotlight. The people in the first row began to turn around as well. Now she had all eyes on her.

The men, two burly gorillas who looked like they'd been made to keep people out of places like this, blocked her way. Before they did, though, she caught sight of the director, Pietro. His eyes flooded with recognition. *"Pazza! Assassina!"*

Oh, no. That's definitely not good.

One of the men blocking her way reached for her. She dodged backwards and down a row. Bea squealed, "Mom!"

"I know this is a closed rehearsal, but I have something to say!" she called as the men stalked after her. She picked up the pace, rushing across one of the rows, toward another aisle. "I know who murdered Marcello Camillo! It was one of your actors, and he's here right now!"

She got to the aisle before the men in the nearer rows did, and sprinted past them. One of them lunged for her, missed, and stumbled forward, letting out a booming *oof.* The other one stumbled over him and sprinted for Diana. Diana's blood went cold and she bolted to the stage.

Bea, lingering a few rows back, groaned. "Just tell them, Mom. We are *so* going to jail after this."

Diana's face was red. She couldn't breathe. A massive, painful stitch was building in her side. She sincerely doubted Hercule Poirot ever had this kind of trouble during one of his reveals. She could feel the burly security guard on her back. There was no place to go, except . . .

She rushed to the staircase on the side of the arena and climbed up to the stage, tripping over her own feet, so blurry was her vision. Her head spun from the heat, and the feeling of all eyes on her. She felt crazy. She probably *looked* crazy. Just like she had in Paris, when she'd climbed into a man's house to find a necklace. She'd come up empty then. She could only hope her intuition was right this time. Otherwise . . . she'd be thrown in prison, and Vidal would find a *lot* to laugh about, then.

Whoever was running the spotlights put one on her, maybe to turn her into a deer in headlights. She blinked and shielded her eyes, trying to catch her breath. "Please . . . I just have something to say! I know who killed Marcello Camillo!"

The director was on his feet now, lumbering forward and shouting directions to the security guards and into his headset. *"You!"* he shouted up at her. "We do not need to listen to you at all. You are the murderer! And the police are on their way to remove you!"

Bea covered her face with her hands. "Nice going, Mom."

"Security! Remove this woman! The play will never go on with her here!" Then he looked up toward the heavens, tossed his clipboard on the ground, and mumbled what had to have been Italian curses.

The security guards got into position, one on either side of the stage. They advanced toward her. There was nowhere to go now.

"Oberon!" she shouted, locating him in the crowd of actors who'd appeared on stage to watch the commotion. "Alfonzo Rivalta! The actor who played Oberon in yesterday's production. He's the killer."

All eyes shifted from Diana to him.

136

He held up his hands, taking in the suspicious glares of the people near him. Then he looked back at Diana. "What? Are you mad?"

"You played Oberon yesterday, but you weren't going to play him tonight, were you?" Diana said. "That's because someone else took the part of Oberon from you. Marcello. He asked Pietro for it, and Pietro gave it to him."

She glanced at Pietro, who nodded. He motioned the security guards to stop advancing on her, and the next time he spoke, his voice was quieter. "Yes. I did."

"And Alfonzo was upset, wasn't he?" Diana said, pleased that now, at least some of the people were listening to her. "I know that when I was backstage last night, I heard Pietro arguing. I didn't see who it was with, but it was Alfonzo, wasn't it?"

Pietro nodded, his round face growing red. "That is right."

Now all eyes were on Alfonzo. Alfonzo shook his head. "This is madness. Pure madness. Why would I kill Marcello? For a stupid part?"

Behind her, Mariana spoke up. "You've always been jealous of Marcello, Alfonzo. Admit it. You complained constantly that he was taking your parts."

His eyes went wide. "Yes, but . . ." He pulled on the collar of his linen blouse. "How could I do that? And when? I didn't—"

"You're a smoker," Mariana announced. "You had the lighter on you."

Diana nodded. "You could have easily popped the cork with the lighter while he was onstage, put the poison in, and jammed the cork back in without being seen."

Now the security guards were backing away from Diana and heading toward Alfonzo, who was backing away from all of them. "This is insane. Absolutely insane. You have no proof."

Just then, the police burst in through the doors at the back of the theater. With that sudden movement, while all eyes turned to watch them, Alfonzo seized the moment. He spun around and rushed for the back exit.

CHAPTER TWENTY THREE

Diana gasped. "He's getting away!" Bea shouted, pointing.

Security guards and police alike swarmed into the back of the theater, after the culprit. Diana, still winded after her last jaunt, rushed after them. As she got to the back room, she found him, holding up his hands in surrender. "I'm innocent!" he shouted. *"Innocente!"*

"Tell that to the police," Bea muttered, coming up behind Diana. Then she smiled at her mom. "Good work, Sherlock."

She smiled at her daughter. "I couldn't have done it without my right hand, Dr. Watson."

"Good." She rubbed her stomach. "So now can we get some food? I'm about to pass out."

"Not just yet," Diana said. After her adventures in Paris, Diana knew that the police would have plenty of questions, i's to dot and t's to cross, so she and Bea stood off to the side, waiting to be excused from the crime scene.

Bea groaned.

Most everyone seemed shocked to find that a member of their troupe had resorted to murder. No one spoke, or if they did, it was in hushed tones. The only exception was, of course, Alfonzo, who was screaming in Italian, loudly professing his innocence to everyone who could hear as the police cuffed him and carted him away.

"That was exciting," Bea admitted as Alfonzo, flanked by officers, disappeared from view.

"You didn't expect that from such a goody-goody, did you?" She pinched her daughter's side.

"Not at all. There's hope for you yet, Mom." Bea watched the space where she'd last seen Alfonzo with wide eyes. "Wow, he's a really good actor, don't you think? I almost believe he's innocent."

Diana nudged her. "Don't say that."

"I'm not saying anything!" Bea laughed. "I was just kidding. Obviously, it's him. All the pieces fit."

But Diana had to admit, if Alfonzo was guilty, his performance professing his innocence was legendary. If he was innocent, and if she'd made a mistake . . .

No. She wouldn't allow herself to think about that. Alfonzo was the man. She was sure of it. Mariana had been sure. Pietro, too. They all seemed to know he was the culprit. It made sense.

"I think we can probably go—" she said, just as Detective Lucci spotted them and jogged over.

"Signora St. James. What is this I hear about you hearing the suspect arguing with the victim prior to the murder?"

She shook her head. "Oh, no. I didn't. Alfonzo was arguing with Pietro, the director. He was upset about losing the part to Marcello. So he sneaked into his room during the play, opened the bottle with his lighter, and put the poison in."

He raised an eyebrow. "He confessed to that?"

"No . . ." Was he doubting her? After Bea's words, and now his, she had to admit, she was starting to second-guess herself. "But come on. He had the motive. He had the opportunity. And—"

"And not only that," Bea put in, "when she accused him, he tried to run away. What more could you want?"

Diana nodded, hoping that would be enough to convince him. But the detective rubbed his grizzled jaw, as if he was still trying to puzzle it out. "Proof. I need better proof than that," he said, closing his notebook. "We searched all the dressing rooms and didn't find anything to incriminate him. And when we interviewed him, he didn't raise suspicions at all."

"Well, he wouldn't, would he?" Bea said. "He's an actor. Aren't they used to keeping calm under pressure?"

Detective Lucci shrugged. "Maybe. No matter. We'll bring him in for questioning and see if we can squeeze a confession out of him."

"So you mean he isn't under arrest?" Bea asked.

"Oh, he is. For now. But right now, we won't have evidence to keep him." He nodded at each of them in turn, and headed away.

So much for a thank you, good job, Diana thought bitterly as they watched him leave.

Bea clutched at her stomach. "Lily's texted me about three hundred times. *Now*, can we—"

Just then, the director approached them. There was something different about him that Diana couldn't quite put her finger on. After a moment, it came to her. *Oh, right. He's actually smiling at me.*

He bowed humbly to her. "Signora St. James, I apologize for my terrible treatment of you. Please accept my sincerest apologies."

She held out a hand. "No. Really, it's no need."

"As you probably don't know, a cancelled performance, even for just one night . . . it is devastating! A catastrophe! Because of you, our show can go on tonight as planned!" he said with great excitement, his beady eyes gleaming.

"You have enough actors to play for the ones who are missing?"

He nodded. "Oh, *si*. Is no problem. The first night—it was a nightmare. Even with Marcello, it was missing something. But I think I found out what it was. Chemistry. Sizzle. Luca Castille is one of my best players. He always wants to play all the roles. Now he gets the chance to play multiple roles besides Nick Bottom. He will be Oberon, King of the Fairies, too, and he will love it. The audience will love it."

"I'm sure they will. And I'm glad it all worked out for you."

He reached for her hand and clasped it between his two sweaty mitts. "Please, I must have you and your family be my guests for the performance tonight. It is only because of you that this show will go on."

Bea coughed, clearing her throat loudly, and Diana knew exactly what that meant. *Mom, I would rather die than see that play.*

Diana shook her head. "Honestly, I think I might have had enough theater to last me for a long while. But thank you. I appreciate the gesture."

He shrugged. "Well, if you change your mind, there will be a ticket at the box office, waiting for you. *Si?* I will put it under your name. Front row seat, eh?"

She nodded. "Yes. Again, thank you."

They watched the man plod away toward the stage and call for the actors to assemble. The show was going to go on, and Diana had made it happen. Even though she never wanted to see *A Midsummer Night's Dream* again, she smiled.

At that moment, Bea's stomach growled loudly. "The beast is about to be unleashed."

Diana laughed and took her daughter's hand. "You poor thing. We can't let you waste away. Let's go get you something to eat."

140

"That was absolutely *crazy*," Bea said for the hundredth time as they made their way into the villa. "I really thought you were done for, Mom."

The second Diana pushed open the door, she was pounced upon by her eldest child. "Where have you been?" she cried. "And done for, what? What does that mean?"

Diana opened her mouth to tell her it was nothing, water under the bridge, but Bea said, "Oh my God. We had the craziest afternoon. Mom nearly got arrested and wound up catching the murderer of that actor."

Lily's jaw dropped. "*Our* mom?"

Diana again attempted to soften the severity of the situation she'd been in, but before she could get any words out, Bea said, "Yep. It was cool. She was masterful! A regular Sherlock."

"*Mom* was?" Lily asked, confused.

"Yep. She used her little gray cells like Hercule Poirot and solved the whole mystery!" Bea said as Evan appeared at the top of the steps.

"What's this?" he asked, jogging down with his hands in the pockets of his bathing trunks, a linen shirt open almost to his navel. At least he'd lost the ridiculous hat. "Di, don't tell me you were putting yourself in harm's way."

Bea went on, gushing, "It was actually kind of like the ending to *Three Act Tragedy*, where Poirot nailed the poisoning actor right in the theater. He made a break for it, and the police swarmed in and caught him!"

"Wow," Lily said in awe. "Who did it?"

Diana finally beat Bea to the punch. "It was an actor named Alfonzo Rivalta. It appears he was jealous of the victim because he'd taken the part he wanted to play."

"And *you* caught him?" Evan asked, eyebrows raised.

She nodded, beaming proudly.

"*You?*" he said again, as if he hadn't heard her right the first time.

Her smile fell to a scowl. *Maybe I'm not as helpless and needing of your assistance as you might think, Evan!*

"Yes. Why do you doubt her, Daddy?" Bea snapped. "You should've seen it! Mom was magnificent!" Bea wrapped an arm around her mother and hugged her tight.

Lily winced. "Really? Jealous? God. What a silly thing for someone to commit murder for!"

"I don't think so. People commit murder over jealousy all the time," Bea said.

"But over losing a part?" Lily asked.

Bea shrugged. "If I was in a group with a bunch of people and someone kept taking credit for everything I did and besting me all the time, I might resort to poisoning, too."

Everyone stared at her.

"Kidding!" she shouted, looking around. "Where's the fiancée?"

Evan, who'd been gazing at Diana all this time in a kind of awe, broke from his trance. "Uh . . . I think she went out to the pool to sunbathe before dinner. I was going to join her. Anyone else want to come along?"

No one volunteered. He frowned.

Bea said, "Sorry. But I need food. Now," and rushed off into the kitchen.

"Guess you're feeling better!" Lily called after her, glaring at Diana. "We had a lovely lunch without you guys. Tilda drank too much, *again*."

Evan coughed. Diana expected he'd cover for her, but instead he rubbed the back of his neck and said, ashamedly, "Yes. It's unfortunate. She does like her cocktails. But we brought her back here and filled her up with espresso, and now she should be just fine."

Diana shrugged innocently and began to follow her Lily when the door to the patio slipped open and Tilda appeared, pulling a silken kimono over her nearly obscene yellow bikini. She fluffed her hair. "*Gawd*, I fell asleep out there! I need an aspirin! I've got *such* a headache!"

She stopped when she saw them all, congregating in the foyer.

Evan smiled. "No problem, darling. I'll get you one."

She ignored him, instead focusing on Diana. "Oh. You're finally back. Is BB all right? When we got home and you weren't here, we thought you might've taken her to the hospital. She looked bad."

Diana blinked. What was that? For once, Vidal was thinking of someone other than herself? "Yes. She's fine. She's in the kitchen, getting something to eat."

Evan said, "Diana was just telling us of the excitement she had today. It turns out, she was of some help to the police. She helped them catch the man who murdered the actor."

Tilda's mouth made an O. "*Gawd*. Really?"

"Yes," Evan said. "It was another actor. Poisoned the man's wine while he was on stage, apparently?"

Diana nodded.

Tilda clapped her hands. "Oh, my *gawd*, that's exciting! Good for you, Diana! Do you think you'll get your picture in the media? Will the press be coming here to interview you?" She started to look around frantically, probably for a hairbrush or a mirror.

"No, probably not."

She sighed in disappointment. "Oh. That's too bad. I can't believe that. Poisoning someone's wine bottle while they aren't looking? It's almost like that . . . what was it? *Romeo and Juliet*!"

Diana smiled. No, not really, except for the poisoning, and them being in Verona. But it was actually a lot closer than she had been. At least she'd actually named a Shakespeare play. "Yes, it was very exciting."

"Well," Evan said, showing her the way to the kitchen. "I'm sure you must be hungry, too. We won't keep you." He smiled at Tilda and turned to jog back up the staircase. "I'll get you that aspirin, dear."

Diana went to her bedroom, got a Band-Aid for her foot, and put it on. By then, the wound was bleeding. After that, she limped into the kitchen, where Bea was sitting at the center island while the housekeeper fussed around the stove. She had a massive bowl of grapes in front of her. "Mom!" she said, patting the stool next to her. "Gaia is going to make her *pasta e fagioli* for us. She says it's her specialty from her hometown."

Gaia looked back and smiled.

"Oh, that sounds like so much trouble," Diana said, sitting next to her. "Are you sure?"

"She says it's no trouble. She had it ready." Bea passed the bowl over to her. "Have a grape."

Gaia pulled two bowls down from a cabinet. "*Vino?*"

Diana nodded, and the housekeeper poured them two glasses of red. As she did, Diana thought about what Tilda had said. *Poisoning someone's wine bottle while they aren't looking.* As she drew the glass toward her, something tickled at the back of her mind, something that didn't quite sit right.

She took a sip, savoring the taste on her tongue.

When had Alfonzo poisoned the wine? She'd seen him arguing with the director about the following night's performance, but that was right before she'd gone into Marcello's room. So that meant that the bottle had to have been poisoned prior to that.

And . . . likely, prior to him finding out that he wasn't going to play Oberon the following night.

So the motive she thought he had . . . really wasn't a motive at all.

She straightened her back. *Oh no.* So that meant that Alfonzo probably couldn't have killed Marcello.

Big mistake.

"Mom? Are you okay? You just went sheet white."

"Yes," she said, touching her face. Her skin was cold, but that wasn't worrying her at the moment. At the time that the poison had been put into Marcello's bottle, the only people who knew about the role change would've been Marcello, and . . .

Of course.

She sprang up from the counter. "I've got to go."

"Where? Mom!" Bea shouted as Diana headed for the door. "What's wrong? Should I come with you?"

"No. You're hungry, Watson. You've done enough. Everything's fine," she called over her shoulder. "You stay here and enjoy."

She reached the front door and threw it open. She had to make it to the theater as soon as possible.

CHAPTER TWENTY FOUR

By this time, Diana had been to the theater so many times she could've found it in her sleep. That was a good thing, because daylight was waning. As she rushed up the main road, she became entangled in the crowds of theater-goers, all heading for the open doors of the arena.

Impatient, Diana waited in a line at the box office. When she got to the ticket counter, she said, "There should be a ticket here for me? St. James?"

The man behind the glass went through a file folder and pulled one out. *"Si . . .e goditi lo spettac—"* he said, sliding it across to her.

She snatched it before he could finish the sentence. *"Grazie!"*

The Band-Aid on her foot wasn't helping as much as she liked. Limping toward the theater area, she found herself caught in the crowds. An usher tried to thrust a program in her hands, but she waved it away. All of them were heading toward the right, and the general admission area. Diana broke off and swerved to the left. As she arrived at the entry toward the backstage area, she came across the same old man who'd been there before.

"Uh, hello," she said, wondering how she was going to finagle admission.

The man smiled at her. "I remember you. The American!"

"Yes, you remember? I was the one to visit yesterday."

He nodded. "Yes, you were the one with the origami rose, eh?"

She reached into her pocket and pulled out the rose, but this one was the one that had been for Linda. "That's right!"

She held her breath, sure that he'd make the connection that Marcello was dead and in no way could be in any condition to visit with groupies. But he simply pushed off his stool, hobbled to the side, and motioned her forward. "Downstairs. End of hall. Right."

"Grazie!" she shouted again, rushing down the darkened hall. When she got far enough along it and heard the voices of the actors, she slowed, wishing she had a disguise. As she went past the first door, which was open this time, she peered inside.

145

It wasn't a dressing room. It was an office. On the door, written in chalk, was the name *P. Samboca.*

Pietro. The director.

She inched closer, scanning the room. It was a mess, the desk piled high with papers. There was no obvious décor except for a wilting fern in the corner. Other than the desk, an old ripped chair, bleeding stuffing, and a massive floor safe, there wasn't much else in the room.

She paused there, glancing down the hallway. Likely, Pietro was making preparations for the performance. She'd be safe.

At least, she hoped she'd be safe.

Taking a deep breath, she quickly went inside, scanning the disaster that was his desk. Pulling on the chain of a banker's lamp, she took in the mess, absently paging through scripts, piles of receipts, menus for local restaurants, old programs from previous performances, all thrown together in a mish-mash, with no organization whatsoever. The room was a haze of dust and an unpleasant stench, like mold, body odor, and garbage.

She realized where at least part of that smell had come from when she tilted her head and found a garbage can full of paper take-out containers.

She sighed, hardly knowing where to begin, but the next time she breathed in, her nose tickled. She tried to stifle the sneeze, but it erupted. Once. Twice. Dust puffed out from around her face. Her eyes watered. She didn't know what she was looking for, but she felt sure that she would know it when she found it.

Holding her breath, she shifted aside some of the papers, and then she saw it.

A piece of paper, folded into the shape of a sailboat.

On the front of it was only one word: *Pietro.*

Heart thumping in her chest, she lifted it up and was about to open it when a large form darkened the space in the doorway.

She stiffened as the director's low, raspy voice said, "What are you doing here? You don't belong here! How did you get here?"

Courage, Diana. Gripping the note in her hand, she came around the desk. "I know. I just realized, after thinking it over, that I made a mistake. About Alfonzo."

He stared at her, eyes narrowed. Down the hallway, footsteps sounded. He was momentarily distracted by them, but then turned back

146

to her. "This is not the time, nor the place, Signora St. James. I think you know that."

"I think Alfonzo will think it's the perfect time," she said. "For the truth."

Pietro shook his head as she approached. He moved aside, but only to let her go out to the lobby. He blocked her from the other actors as he pointed forcefully toward the exit. "Go. Before I have to call security."

She stepped out into the hall. Beyond the body of Pietro, as wide as it was, she could see other actors, who must've heard the commotion, because they were turned her way. "Not before you tell me when it was you put the poison into Marcello's bottle."

He stared at her in horror. "What? You know Alfonzo did that."

"He couldn't have. That's what I realized. He didn't have time. At the time you told Alfonzo that he wouldn't be playing Oberon at today's performance, the poison had to have already been in the bottle. He was with Mariana, and then with me, and the bottle was in his dressing room the whole time. There was no time for Alfonzo to put the poison in the bottle."

He scowled. "You're crazy. Leave this place at once."

He turned to go back to the stage, but there were already several actors standing there, watching him. Mariana and Luca were among them.

"Not until I read this," Diana said, holding up the note. "I know it was from Marcello, because it's folded this way."

Pietro gaped.

She carefully unfolded the note and read the words. Or, she tried to read the words. Unfortunately, they were all in Italian. "Um . . ."

"Let me see!" Mariana said, pushing past Pietro and snatching the letter. "It says, *'Pietro. I know what you have done. Time to pay for your past mistakes.'"*

She looked up and Luca gasped.

A grin spread over Diana's face. *A-ha! I was right!*

Mariana's eyes went wide. She said, "Oh my god. I'm just remembering. A couple days ago, Marcello told me he had something to talk to you about. I thought it was changing a part. But . . . it was this, wasn't it? He was blackmailing you for . . . oh my god!" She covered her mouth with her hand. "And you *killed* him for that?"

147

"This is outrageous," he blustered, shaking his head. "I have done nothing wrong. Alfonzo has already been arrested for this crime. He's the killer."

Luca shook his head. "No. I know what this is about. We say we are a family but I always had it in my mind that something was off. And Marcello always said there were things about you, Pietro, that were not what they seemed. Was he blackmailing you for the role?"

He shook his head. "I will not say another word. The show. It must go on!"

"Without you, it looks like," the old security guard stated, ambling up behind Diana. He reached for his radio. "I'm calling the police."

Pietro laughed. "That's ridiculous! I am this show! Don't you see? It's all because of me our troupe is so renowned. You will fail! All of you! You need me."

By now, more actors were coming out of their dressing rooms in full costume, watching him sadly. Luca said, "I think we will do just fine without you, Signore," and waved him goodbye.

Diana stood there, stunned by the way all of his "family" suddenly seemed to turn on him, waving him off. Something still seemed off about this. A piece of the puzzle was missing. She'd been too rash before. She didn't want to make the same mistake.

"Wait. Please. Yes, it seems that Marcello was blackmailing him for the part of Oberon. But . . . what did Marcello know that Pietro was willing to kill him to silence him for? I don't understand that part."

Mariana cleared her throat. "I think I might be able to help clear that up."

CHAPTER TWENTY FIVE

All heads swung to Titania, who suddenly looked smaller than ever in her resplendent, golden fairy gown.

She met Pietro's eyes for a long time before taking a breath, as if readying herself to speak a long monologue. "I am not proud to admit this, but years ago, Pietro made me an offer I couldn't refuse. He offered me a spot on *Compagnia del Andre*, in exchange for certain favors . . ."

She shook her head, hanging it in shame. Behind her, Luca put a hand on her shoulder. She put a hand over his and smiled sadly.

When she spoke again, her voice was quieter. "Sexual favors. Of course, I was young and naïve and wanted to be an actress more than anything, and I saw it as my only way. And unfortunately, it didn't end once I made a name for myself. It continued on. Marcello found out . . . about a week ago. I must've had too much to drink and admitted it to him. Pietro has a wife, a family. He knows that should that information get out, it would destroy him, both personally and professionally."

Diana's stomach twisted. This was all so wretched. "So Marcello intended to go public with this information if he didn't get the parts he wanted?"

Mariana shook her head. "I don't think so. He never would've done such a thing. He just wanted the beast to pay. And he knew how to hit Pietro where it hurt."

Angry and disgusted faces turned to the director. Avoiding them, Pietro raised his eyes to the ceiling and let out a long breath of air. "This is ludicrous."

"You deny that?" Mariana questioned in shock.

"Utterly," he said, his voice faint. "This is slander. And you no longer have a job in this company."

She laughed. "You're forgetting, Pietro? I have plenty of proof. All those videos you insisted on taking, never realizing that I took some of my own . . ."

His eyes went wide, then shifted to the right and left.

People began muttering at him in Italian. Diana couldn't understand the words, but from the tone, they sounded like insults. Someone said, "I am sick when I do look on thee," and another shouted, "I'd beat thee, but I would infect my hands."

Ah, *Shakespearean* insults. Even better.

Suddenly, he burst forward, knocking over the old security guard and rushing, as fast as his stubby legs could carry him, down the hall. For someone so large, he was fast. He made it down the hallway, heading for the stage, in the blink of an eye, bowling over a couple of fairies who were standing there and disappearing from view.

"Get him!" Diana shouted, but everyone around her was glued to their spot in the hallway, still frozen in shock. Diana broke into a run after him, tearing down the hallway, only remembering the pain in her foot when it shot up her ankle, to her knee. She winced and shouted after the stagehand. "Someone call the police!"

Luca was the first to break into action after Diana, rushing behind her, with Mariana on his heels. As Diana skidded to a stop at the end of the hall, a spotlight blinded her. Luca pointed. "He went that way!"

She limped forward, following his pointed finger, and suddenly emerged from the bright light as a murmur of voices rose up. She pushed aside the curtains and raced forward, finding herself . . .

She froze.

She was on the stage.

In the audience, most of the people had already taken their seats, and it was a full house. The murmuring slowly died as once again, a spotlight fell on her. Eyes shifted to watch her, as if she was part of the entertainment.

Luca and Mariana joined her on stage, one on each side of her. They were much more comfortable with it, clearly, because Luca didn't hesitate. "Over there! Behind the tree."

Sure enough, Pietro was standing behind a piece of scenery, trying to catch his breath. When they focused on him and started to advance, he dodged them, heading for the other side of the stage. "There's no way out there," Mariana said.

Luca nodded and motioned to her. "You go around back. Diana, you block the stairs so he doesn't go down. I'll get him." Diana did what she was told, moving to the stairs. As she took her place, Luca called, "There's no way out, Pietro. Give it up."

Mariana came near him, and he quickly stumbled away. As Luca moved in, he moved off, somehow evading him. For someone so big, he was definitely slippery and spry. It almost looked like a comic act, Laurel and Hardy doing their slapstick humor. That was probably why the audience began to laugh whenever he slipped from Luca's grip. He faked one way, then ran another, slipping on the slick surface of the stage. The audience burst into laughter and clapped at the zany antics. People wolf-whistled and shouted for more.

A spotlight began to follow his every move, making the sweat on his brow glisten. Crouching behind a gazebo, still panting, he surveyed his escape options. Diana thought for sure he'd realize that he was done. But Pietro had much more fight in him than she'd anticipated, because suddenly, he bolted around another tree, straight for Luca.

Luca held his arms out, but Pietro suddenly sprang forward, delivering a right hook to the jaw that leveled Luca, sending him falling hard, unconscious before he even hit the stage. On the stage, Mariana gasped. People shouted wildly. They must've been wondering how the fight scenes could look so real.

Without warning, Pietro wheeled around and headed straight for Diana. And the closer her got, the more speed he picked up, until she knew there was no time for him to stop. "Stand back, *strega*."

Diana braced herself and closed her eyes as he shoved into her, sending her sprawling backwards down the stairs, hitting the steps on her backside and one of her arms. The pain in her elbow was exquisite. As she tumbled down the rest of the stone steps, she reached a hand out, grasping the cuff of his pants. She heard a terrible tear as he shook his leg, trying to extract himself from her grip.

She didn't let go. She engaged in a tug-of-war with him, desperate to keep him there, until she felt the fabric slowly giving loose. "Let go! Let go, you *mucca*!"

"No. You will stay right here!" she ordered, in a voice that didn't sound like herself.

He growled something in Italian and kicked at her hand, then reached over, trying to pry her fingers off the hem of his pants.

She held on for as long as she could, but unfortunately, it wasn't enough to slow him. The piece of fabric slipped from her fingers, and he continued down the steps, hitting the ground with a mighty thud. The audience must have thought this was some strange pre-show event, because they began to clap in time as he lumbered his way up the aisle.

151

Lying on the third step of the staircase, out of breath and nursing her sore elbow, she called, "Stop him! Someone, please! He's getting away!"

But nobody did. Either they didn't speak English, or they thought it was part of the show. They all sat there in their seats, clapping and laughing, while the murderer disappeared, possibly forever.

Still stunned from the fall, she raised her head, but she could only manage to get it up a few inches before she fell back in pain. On the stage, Luca was absolutely still. Only Mariana stood there, at the edge of the stage, shouting something in Italian. Whatever it was, it had no effect.

Diana watched helplessly as Pietro hurried toward the back of the theater and the lobby. It was probably too soon for the police to have arrived. In another few steps, he'd be gone. The real murderer, gone.

Just as he was about to disappear from view, he let out a horrible grunt and stumbled backwards.

CHAPTER TWENTY SIX

Diana pulled herself upright and squinted to get a better look. There, she saw Bea, shaking her sore hand. Had she . . . punched Pietro in the face? Where had she learned a thing like that? Certainly not from her.

Was she hallucinating? Or was that her entire family . . . forming an impenetrable barrier, keeping the killer from fleeing?

"Dad. Get him!" Bea shouted in a war cry that echoed through the theater. "He just shoved Mom down the steps, the jerk!"

Evan reached forward and grabbed him by the collar. "What do you think you're doing?" he shouted.

"Yeah!" Lily shouted, smacking him across the face like a jilted debutante. "That's our mother you're messing with."

Even Tilda got in on the action, stepping forward and grounding her stiletto heel into his toes. He howled.

Evan grabbed him and shoved him forward, down the aisle, toward Diana. The four members of her family and Tilda formed a united front, a wall, behind Pietro, so that there was nowhere for him to escape to. Face red, breathing hard, he hung his head, finally accepting defeat.

Evan gave her his hand and helped her up. She clutched her sore elbow and smiled. "Looks like you were just in time. How did you know where to find me?"

Bea laughed. "Lucky guess. Since we've only been here about a hundred times in the last day, I had a feeling." She motioned to Pietro. "So is this the real killer?"

Diana nodded. This time, nothing tickled at the back of her head, telling her she'd made a mistake. This time, she was sure.

The police swarmed in shortly afterward, just around the time when the audience started to understand that this wasn't a part of the show. The cheers and laughter gave way to shocked silence and murmurs. Diana slumped in a chair in the back row of the theater, away from the fray, watching the police escort Marcello's murderer out to the lobby.

I would kill for a glass of wine, she thought, then cringed. Pietro had killed *with* a glass of wine. Maybe a glass of water would be better.

153

The audience had been dismissed pending the investigation, and were told that they would receive communication soon about the next performance. Detective Lucci approached her while she was sitting there, trying to calm herself down. He handed her a bottle of water.

She smiled gratefully. "Are you going to let Alfonzo Rivalta go?" she asked.

He nodded. "Already did, a couple hours ago. He checked out."

"Oh, that's wonderful. I feel terrible for accusing him."

"Looks like we finally got the right person, though. You said you found a letter?"

She handed him the folded note. "Yes. Here it is."

"How did you make the connection?"

"It occurred to me that if Alfonzo was arguing with Pietro about the part, it was the first he was hearing about it. He didn't have time to go into Marcello's dressing room and slip the poison in."

"Ah. I see. And we already have a statement from Mariana. It turns out, this director had a long history of demanding certain favors from the female players. But this time, he got caught." He shrugged and closed the notebook in his hand. "So I guess this case is closed. Thanks for your help. I think I may have misjudged you."

She smiled. "You're welcome."

"But that doesn't mean I need your help in any other investigations. You're leaving soon?"

She nodded. "Yes. In a few days."

"Good." He winked, straightened, and headed for the exit.

Luca, with some of the other actors, waved at her and jogged over. "That gives new meaning to the phrase, 'bringing down the house,' eh?"

She winced. "I am sorry if I ruined your production."

He laughed. "Don't be silly! We are all talking that we are better off without that rascal Pietro. He was always going around, making decisions that make no sense. Now we know why. We think *Compagnia del Andre* will be even better off now without him. And I get to try my hand at directing now, too!" He nudged her arm. "So I should be thanking you."

"Oh, that's great. But what about *A Midsummer Night's Dream*?"

"We think it'll go on tomorrow night. Better than ever. With plenty of chemistry, *si*? I'll be playing Bottom, Oberon . . . now I really get to stretch my acting muscles!" He laughed.

154

"That's great. I'm glad it worked out."

He nodded. "You want tickets for tomorrow?"

She shook her head. "As much as I enjoyed your acting, I think I'd better stick to spending the rest of this vacation with my family. I've been neglecting them. But I appreciate the offer."

"Not a problem. *In bocca al lupo! Buona fortuna!* May your journeys be safe and may I see you in our fair city once again, one day.*"* He took her hand and, with all the drama of the great actor he was, kissed her knuckles. She blushed.

The second he left, Bea swooped in, holding an ice pack over her bruised knuckles. She looked at the man, wide-eyed. "Another admirer?"

Diana laughed. Luca was at the most, half her age, and though Evan might have been interested in dating younger, Diana had little interest in that. Plus, there was the matter of David. "Sorry, no."

Bea looked around the near-empty arena in distaste. "Well, I always thought I hated theater, but now I *know* I do. That was definitely an adventure."

"I thought you *liked* adventure."

"Depends on what kind. How is your elbow?"

Diana pulled back her sleeve and looked at it. It was just a little red. "Fine. Hardly hurts at all anymore. Your hand?"

Bea frowned. "Now I know I don't want to be a boxer when I grow up," she said with a laugh. "That was exhausting. I want to go to bed and never wake up."

"When do you leave?"

"Oh. I have to take the red-eye, the night after tomorrow." Her brows tented. "Hai texted me an hour ago. Said he had something important to tell me."

"Good! See, he's not ignoring you."

"Yeah, I think it's something bad."

"Oh, nonsense. How do you know?"

"I think he wants to break up with me. I just get that vibe, with how weird and secretive he'd been acting. I get the feeling there's someone else." Her lower lip protruded in a definite pout. She sighed. "But I guess I can't hide here forever. I have to go back to Japan and face the music eventually."

Diana patted her hand. "Try not to get too worked up over it. Just think, we have another two whole days to explore the town before we say goodbye. That'll be fun, right? I'd love to—"

Bea yawned. "Oh, you had me running all over Verona. I don't know if I can keep up with you, Sherlock. Maybe we just take it easy and relax a little?"

Diana smiled. Yes, they could take it easy and reconnect. She didn't need to take any fancy tours of places she could see in books or movies, because that wasn't what made travel special. She'd gone on a few tours in Paris, and barely remembered much of the major landmarks she'd seen. What she did remember were the little, unexpected things that happened to her on the way—the people she met, the unique, off-the-beaten-path places she'd stopped in, the culture that she'd been immersed in. A little relaxation at the villa, maybe some good food and a few strolls around town, would be perfect.

Just being in Italy with the people she loved was enough.

*

The following morning, as was her usual routine, Diana woke early. She showered and changed, expecting to go downstairs and spend a quiet morning, before anyone was up, enjoying the sun on the patio or chatting with Gaia while she made breakfast.

She found Gaia there, preparing breakfast, but when she looked out onto the patio, she also saw Evan, sitting in the sun with his coffee, reading the newspaper.

That was odd. Evan was a late sleeper when he didn't have to work, just like Bea. At first, Diana assumed maybe Tilda had changed his ways, but when she scanned the patio, she didn't see his fiancée.

"Oh, Signora St. James," Gaia said, ushering her toward the French doors to the patio. "Go on out and keep Signore St. James company. I was just about to serve breakfast."

"Are you sure I can't help?"

"Yes, of course," she said, motioning faster to her. Then she winked. "The whole town is abuzz with news of the murder that was solved at the arena last night. Your daughter said you had something to do with it?"

"Not very much," Diana said, but it was reason enough for her to move quickly outside. After all the questions she'd had to answer for

156

the police last night, she really didn't want to go into it anymore. The chapter of Marcello Camillo's murder had come to an end, and soon, so would her adventures in Italy.

When she slid open the door, Evan dipped the newspaper in his lap and looked up. A smile appeared on his face. "Good morning, love."

The poor fool was happy to see her. Maybe he really had thought that all of them being together would be harmless, a way to get together all of his family while making sure Diana was taken care of. He'd done silly things like that before, things that defied logic. Even though he never seemed to think things through, his heart had always been in the right place.

Folding his paper and setting it aside, he pushed out a chair next to him and said, "Sit. Gaia's making breakfast. I'm famished. How about you?"

"I could eat," she said, sitting. "I'm surprised to see you up. You were never the early bird, from what I remember. Turning over a new leaf?"

He shook his head. "Honestly, I couldn't sleep at all last night. I realized early this morning that it was because I haven't said what I need to say to you."

Gaia came out and poured her coffee, topping off Evan's. Diana dragged the cup and saucer to her and said, "Oh?"

"Well, yes. I know you must have all sorts of feelings about me and Tillie, marrying. And I understand them. They're warranted. I don't for a second think that what she and I will have will be anything like what I shared with you." He sighed. "The thing is, I think of the times you and I used to curl up on the couch together and read. That was nice. Tillie's more likely to drag me out to a dance club."

She stared at him. Did he think he was going to shock her by stating that she and Tilda were nothing alike? That was something she'd known from the first moment. "I'm sorry, I don't understand."

"I guess, well . . . I know you can take care of yourself just fine, Di, and you'll probably be better off without me. That was just my excuse. The reason I came out here with the family is because, well . . . I miss us." His face reddened with embarrassment. "All of us, together, as a family."

Her eyes widened. "Evan . . . you're marrying Tilda."

"Yes, I know that, I know that," he said quickly. "And I love Tilda. But I thought back to the times we were all together and I love that, too.

157

I guess what I'm saying is that even though I'm happy to be creating a life with Tilda, it doesn't mean I want to leave you all behind. You're all still my family, even you, Diana. I will always care for you."

Diana put a hand on his. "Evan—"

"I'm not an idiot. I know what people say about Tillie. I know she will likely run me ragged and that in a lot of ways, we're night and day. I know it won't be easy for you all to accept her, and I probably shouldn't be asking you to, considering what I put you through. I promised 'til death do us part, and I failed. So you have every right to hate me. But of anyone on this Earth, Diana, it was always your opinion that meant the most to me. So I guess what I'm asking you, what I'm hoping, is that you can find it in your heart to . . . not hate me?"

She let out a sigh. "Evan. Please. I don't hate you. Not even a little bit," she said honestly. "At first, yes, I was a little shocked. I think I do know you better than most people, and someone like Tilda, well . . . I suppose I never saw her fitting in your life. But I see she makes you happy, now. And that's great. If this marriage is what you want and will continue your happiness, then I think it's wonderful. We must all chase our happiness, right?"

He nodded. "That's right. And I want every happiness for you, too, Di. From the bottom of my heart. Part of me thought that you might have been running away from something because of what I did to you, but now I see, this trip has been good for you. I see you've changed, become more of your own person. And yes, I think you're happier. That's what I want for all of my family. And you'll always be my family." He held her hand. "So I was hoping that you would come to the wedding? Possibly this Christmas, but I'm not sure. Tilda's in charge of the planning."

Diana shrugged. "Well, I hope to still be touring Europe, but that's around when Lily's baby will be due. I'm planning to come back to the States for that. So put me down as a definite maybe?"

He nodded and smiled. "A definite maybe. Yes. I think that will be good, Diana. Though I'm afraid that another few months out here and maybe you'll never want to leave."

"You're forgetting . . . in another few months, I'll have a grandchild to come home to," she said as Gaia arrived with their food, plates full of eggs and pastries and tomatoes from the vast garden on the side of the villa.

Yes, she had changed. A few months ago, she couldn't imagine being a grandmother. The thought of aging with a failed marriage while Evan went off and experienced a second youth was almost too much to bear. But now, it seemed right. She no longer felt like she was being left behind while everyone else moved their lives forward. And now, she felt excited about that chapter of her life.

Just as excited as she was to continue on with her next chapter in her European journey.

CHAPTER TWENTY SEVEN

Two days later, after a nice, relaxing time enjoying the togetherness of her family, it was finally time to separate. No, it hadn't been all sunshine and roses, and yes, Vidal had created quite a few eyeroll-moments, but their lives together never had been perfect. The days of strolling around Italy with her family, enjoying shopping and sights and dinner with them, had been memorable, though, something she would never forget.

She laid her open suitcase on the bed and began to pile it with her belongings, thinking about her next voyage. What country should she tackle next? She knew she'd go north, but there were plenty of places on that bucket list. As she gathered her things and spied her itinerary, she smiled. It was full of all the things she'd wanted to see, but now, as she tucked it into her carry-on, she realized that seeing things in the guidebooks wasn't the most important part.

Not even close.

The old cliché, *It's not the destination, it's the journey,* hung in her head. But it was true. Yes, she'd wanted to see *David* in Florence, but what would it matter if she had? If she'd decided to go north in town to the Accademia to gaze upon it, she might never have run into Evan on the Ponte Vecchio.

And it had been worth it, because at that moment, when she saw him with Tilda, she'd known: She was truly over him.

Whatever thoughts she'd harbored about him realizing his mistake and coming back to her on his knees were gone. She no longer wished that would happen. It had taken a long time to arrive at this place, but now, she knew that while she would always still care for him, whatever she'd had with Evan was truly over, and she was better for it.

It was time to move on to a new adventure. Maybe not one that meant falling in love with another man. Whatever it was, she would be ready for it.

As she was tucking her itinerary away, there was a knock at her door. She turned around to see Bea, holding her duffel bag. "Mommy," she said with a pout. "I have to go. Daddy's driving me to the train station. I have to get to the airport."

Diana went over to her and embraced her tightly, then pulled away and held her innocent, freckled face in her hands, kissing her nose. "I love you, Bea. Please have a safe trip. And please, try not to worry about Hai."

She shook her head. "I haven't been."

That was a lie, but Bea was always one to hide her feelings like that. "All right. Be safe. I will see you again soon. Who knows? Maybe you'll come and visit me again?"

She nodded, her eyes glassy, as if she was going to cry. "Maybe not soon. But I'll definitely be going back to America in December. I have the whole month blocked off! I told Lily I'm coming back to meet my new niece or nephew. And Dad's going to want me there for the wedding." She rolled her eyes.

"Oh, come now," Diana said with a laugh. "Your father is happy. That's all that matters."

Bea gave her mother a surprised look. "Yeah. I guess so. I just wish he hadn't chosen for me a stepmother who thinks Shakespeare wrote *Hamilton*."

Diana laughed. "Definitely December," she said with a smile. "I will miss you. Make sure you call me the second your plane touches down."

"I will. And I love you, too, Mom." She hugged her tightly again. "Bye, Mommy. It's been fun, hasn't it? I mean, aside from nearly being killed and arrested, I had a blast!"

"I did, too." She smiled, her heart heavy with the thought of losing her again. This was the first time she'd seen her daughter in a year, and yet, she'd never felt closer to Bea. It was as if they'd shared more than an adventure together. She learned so much, not only about Italy, but about her daughter and herself, and that was what this trip had been about, after all. "I'm going to miss you, Watson."

Bea giggled. Diana walked her downstairs and outside, where Evan took her bag and put them in the back of the little clown car. She hugged Bea again as she got into the passenger seat, then watched the car as it rode down the driveway and out of sight. The second she was gone, she already missed her.

When she went back upstairs, her heart heavy, she set to the task of finishing her packing. She opened the dresser and pulled out her slacks

161

and shirts, setting them in her bag. She had some of her things in the laundry downstairs, with hopes that she could go on to the next country with a bag full of clean clothes. As she reached into one drawer, pulling out a pair of warm woolen slacks she hadn't worn yet because of the weather, she felt something heavy inside the pocket.

Reaching in, she pulled out her iPhone.

She blinked. How had that gotten there?

She suddenly had a vague memory of putting it into her bag before she'd gotten out of the taxi at the castle in Florence. She'd looked there numerous times, but it must've fallen between her folded clothes and gone into the pocket of her slacks.

I'm so silly, she thought, shaking her head, staring at the dark screen. Of course, the battery was dead. *I've had it with me the whole time.*

For a moment, she was exhilarated, like she usually was when she used to pick up her phone after a long time of not looking at it. That excitement of, *Who is trying to get in touch with me? What have I missed?* sent adrenaline coursing through her veins. She'd never been off the grid for this long. The news of the day, updates from friends, calls and texts and who knew what else? She grabbed her charging cable from her carry-on and quickly plugged it in.

As she waited for it to boot up, that excitement drained. *Actually,* life had been pretty good without that cell phone. Her little flippy thing, while pretty useless, was all she'd needed. It had allowed her to stop and smell the roses, to see the things she sometimes took for granted. And she'd liked that.

She never thought she'd admit it, but she did. She actually liked the idea of letting things go. And maybe that was what this trip was all about. Learning to let things go.

She patted her trusty little flip phone, smiled, and went to yank the cord on her iPhone. As she did, a few missed calls and texts appeared on the display. Mostly unrecognized calls, probably from spammers. But one message stood out among them all. It was a message from Sean, the handsome Irishman she'd met in Paris. He was a drifter, set out upon Europe like a feather on the wind. *How is my American friend's journey so far? Heading north right now to Vienna. Hoping we will connect again soon. Until then, may the wind be at your back!*

She smiled, typed in, *I hope so too!* and stuffed the phone deep into her case. She quite liked having the flip phone by her side instead. Of not driving herself insane preparing for every possible outcome. Of leaving some things to chance and letting the wind take her where it may.

Maybe she would meet Sean again. Maybe not.

But whatever happened, it felt like fate. Meant to be. And even if things went wrong for a time, in the end, everything would be all right.

*

The following morning, bright and early, the four travelers left the villa—Lily, Tilda, and Evan headed for the Verona airport, to catch a flight back to America, and Diana, bound for the train station, to catch a route up north.

"Mom, look at this," Lily said to Diana from the back seat, thrusting her iPhone in front of Diana's face.

It was a text from Bea. It said, *Called Mom but she didn't answer on that little toy phone of hers. Just touched down twenty minutes ago. Show her this!*

It was a picture of Bea's hand, adorned with a lovely, tear-shaped diamond engagement ring.

Diana smiled. "I knew it."

Lily gasped. "Bea and Hai are getting married!" she shouted, mostly so her father could hear. "I can't believe it. I thought she said that it was over between them."

Evan smiled. "Good for them. One day, we'll have to meet the lucky man."

Tilda said, "He'll be at our wedding. I hope they don't decide to tie the knot before we do."

Diana shrugged. All bets were off with Bea, her wild child, the one she'd never been able to predict. Maybe it was hanging out with Bea, these past few days, that had helped Diana to let loose a little. To have fun, even when everything was upside down. She didn't put it past Bea to get married tomorrow, if the mood struck her. On a Ferris wheel. Right before bungee jumping.

She smiled from ear-to-ear, just thinking about how excited and relieved her daughter must've been. *Funny how when good things happen to your children, it's almost more exciting than if they'd happened to you.*

163

When the car stopped at the train station, Diana popped out, ready for the next leg of her journey. She grabbed her bag and hugged Lily tightly, then patted her stomach gently. "Take care of that little peanut. And yourself, okay?"

She smiled. "I love you, Mom."

"I love you, too."

She turned to find Tilda there, holding a shoebox in front of her. Diana hadn't realized she'd gotten out of the car. She looked a little apprehensive as she pushed the box into Diana's hands. "Here. I bought these for you. I saw you struggling a couple days ago, at the Shakespeare Festival, and I thought you could use them."

Confused, Diana opened the lid and looked at them. They were a lovely pair of new shoes. Diana looked up at her, hardly knowing what to say.

"I checked your shoe size while you were out. And Gaia said they're the most comfortable shoes in Italy," she explained.

For the first time, Diana was truly speechless. She was even more so when Tilda wrapped her arms around her and said, "Thanks, Diana. It's been fun. I hope you can make it to our wedding. Until then, have a great trip, and by *gawd*, don't run into any more murderers!"

Still stunned, Diana murmured a thank-you. Evan opened the trunk, and Diana reached in and grabbed her bag before he had a chance to. He looked at her, as if he was about to say something.

She knew this drill. He was going to ask her if she could manage. "I'll be fine," she said, before he could.

"I have no doubt of that," he said with a smile. "Enjoy the rest of your trip. Send us a postcard and let us know where you are."

She laughed. "That depends. Will you follow me there?"

He smiled. "I think I need to be saving up vacation days for the honeymoon. Tillie wants Hawaii. Take care, Di."

"You, too."

Hefting her carry-on over her shoulder, she gave them one last wave. Then she turned, dragged her rolling suitcase down the concourse, and stood in front of the outdoor Departures board. Time to make the all-important decision.

She thought it would be a difficult one. The old Diana would've gone back and forth with the what-ifs. But the answer came to her almost at once.

Vienna, Austria.

164

Yes, that would be absolutely perfect. She'd always wanted to see the great city where Beethoven, Haydn, Brahms, Schubert, Mozart and more were moved to create some of their greatest works. To revel in the opera in one of the most architecturally significant opera houses in the world. To enjoy a Strauss waltz while immersing herself in the culture of the city.

And maybe she would even see her friend Sean again.

That would be interesting.

She rolled her case toward the ticket counter, purchased the ticket, and boarded the train, which seemed to have been sitting there, waiting just for her.

As she settled into her seat, she pulled out her journal and looked at her bucket list item: *Fall in love in Italy.*

No, that hadn't happened. But did it really matter?

Diana decided that it did not. In fact, she'd gotten so much more out of the trip than a romance would've given her.

She crossed out one word and replaced it with another, so that it now read: *Fall in love WITH Italy.*

Yes. Been there, done that. And it had been absolutely everything she'd wanted it to be.

On the next blank page, she wrote the date, and: *On to Vienna, Austria!*

Underneath, she wrote her first bucket-list item for the city: *Be moved to tears by beautiful music.*

Not an easy task. Diana didn't cry much anymore, not after the chain of disappointments in her life. But on this trip, she felt like she was rediscovering the part of herself that she'd deliberately hardened in order to deal with life's upsets. The part that could find enjoyment and pleasure, even through pain and difficulty. The part that could be emotional for *good* reasons, like art or music or beauty.

Yes, she liked that idea very much.

As the train pulled away from the station, Diana took a deep breath and gazed out at the sight of the Italian Alps in the distance. It was breathtaking.

And, for the first time, she allowed her heart to swell fully inside her chest. And as she thought of the trip before her, she prepared herself for tears, unbridled, to come into her eyes.

NOW AVAILABLE!

VENGEANCE IN VIENNA
(A Year in Europe—Book 3)

"When you think that life cannot get better, Blake Pierce comes up with another masterpiece of thriller and mystery! This book is full of twists, and the end brings a surprising revelation. Strongly recommended for the permanent library of any reader who enjoys a very well-written thriller."
--Books and Movie Reviews (re Almost Gone)

VENGEANCE IN VIENNA is book #3 in a charming new cozy mystery series by USA Today bestselling author Blake Pierce, whose #1 bestseller Once Gone has received 1,500 five-star reviews. The series (A YEAR IN EUROPE) begins with book #1 (A MURDER IN PARIS).

Diana Hope, 55, is still adjusting to her recent separation when she discovers her ex-husband has just proposed to a woman 30 years younger. Secretly hoping they would reunite, Diana is devastated. She realizes the time has come to reimagine life without him—in fact, to reimagine her life, period.

Devoting the last 30 years of her life to being a dutiful wife and mother and to climbing the corporate ladder, Diana has been relentlessly driven, and has not taken a moment to do anything for herself. Now, the time has come.

Diana never forgot her first boyfriend, who begged her to join him for a year in Europe after college. She had wanted to go so badly, but it had seemed like a wild, romantic idea, and a gap year, she'd thought, would hinder her resume and career. But now, with her daughters grown, her husband gone, and her career no longer fulfilling, Diana realizes it's time for herself—and to take that romantic year in Europe she'd always dreamed of.

Diana prepares to embark on the year of her life, finally turning to her bucket list, hoping to tour the most beautiful sights and sample the most scrumptious cuisines—and maybe, even, to fall in love again. But a year in Europe may have different plans in store for her. Can A-type Diana learn to go with the flow, to be spontaneous, to let down her guard and to learn to truly enjoy life again?

In VENGEANCE IN VIENNA (Book #3), Diana travels to Vienna, hoping to fulfill her bucket list dream of being moved to tears by music. She is overwhelmed by the beauty, history and culture of the city and wonders if she's finally settling into her trip in Europe—when an unforeseen catastrophe turns her plans upside down. Can Diana investigate her way out of this one?

A YEAR IN EUROPE is a charming and laugh-out-loud cozy mystery series, packed with food and travel, with mysteries that will leave you on the edge of your seat, and with experiences that will leave you with a sense of wonder. As Diana embarks on her quixotic quest for love and meaning, you will find yourself falling in love and rooting for her. You will be in shock at the twists and turns her journey takes as she somehow finds herself at the center of a mystery, and must play amateur sleuth to solve it. Fans of books like Eat, Pray, Love and Under the Tuscan Sun have finally found the cozy mystery series they've been hoping for!

Future books in the series will be available soon.

Did you know that I've written multiple novels in the mystery genre? If you haven't read all my series, download a series starter!

Blake Pierce

Blake Pierce is the USA Today bestselling author of the RILEY PAGE mystery series, which includes seventeen books. Blake Pierce is also the author of the MACKENZIE WHITE mystery series, comprising fourteen books; of the AVERY BLACK mystery series, comprising six books; of the KERI LOCKE mystery series, comprising five books; of the MAKING OF RILEY PAIGE mystery series, comprising six books; of the KATE WISE mystery series, comprising seven books; of the CHLOE FINE psychological suspense mystery, comprising six books; of the JESSE HUNT psychological suspense thriller series, comprising fifteen books (and counting); of the AU PAIR psychological suspense thriller series, comprising three books; of the ZOE PRIME mystery series, comprising six books; of the ADELE SHARP mystery series, comprising ten books (and counting); of the EUROPEAN VOYAGE cozy mystery series, comprising six books (and counting); of the new LAURA FROST FBI suspense thriller, comprising three books (and counting); of the new ELLA DARK FBI suspense thriller, comprising six books (and counting); of the A YEAR IN EUROPE cozy mystery series, comprising three books (and counting); of the AVA GOLD mystery series, comprising three books (and counting); and of the RACHEL GIFT mystery series, comprising three books (and counting).

An avid reader and lifelong fan of the mystery and thriller genres, Blake loves to hear from you, so please feel free to visit www.blakepierceauthor.com to learn more and stay in touch.

BOOKS BY BLAKE PIERCE

RACHEL GIFT MYSTERY SERIES
HER LAST WISH (Book #1)
HER LAST CHANCE (Book #2)
HER LAST HOPE (Book #3)

AVA GOLD MYSTERY SERIES
CITY OF PREY (Book #1)
CITY OF FEAR (Book #2)
CITY OF BONES (Book #3)

A YEAR IN EUROPE
A MURDER IN PARIS (Book #1)
DEATH IN FLORENCE (Book #2)
VENGEANCE IN VIENNA (Book #3)

ELLA DARK FBI SUSPENSE THRILLER
GIRL, ALONE (Book #1)
GIRL, TAKEN (Book #2)
GIRL, HUNTED (Book #3)
GIRL, SILENCED (Book #4)
GIRL, VANISHED (Book 5)
GIRL ERASED (Book #6)

LAURA FROST FBI SUSPENSE THRILLER
ALREADY GONE (Book #1)
ALREADY SEEN (Book #2)
ALREADY TRAPPED (Book #3)

EUROPEAN VOYAGE COZY MYSTERY SERIES
MURDER (AND BAKLAVA) (Book #1)
DEATH (AND APPLE STRUDEL) (Book #2)
CRIME (AND LAGER) (Book #3)
MISFORTUNE (AND GOUDA) (Book #4)
CALAMITY (AND A DANISH) (Book #5)
MAYHEM (AND HERRING) (Book #6)

ADELE SHARP MYSTERY SERIES
LEFT TO DIE (Book #1)

LEFT TO RUN (Book #2)
LEFT TO HIDE (Book #3)
LEFT TO KILL (Book #4)
LEFT TO MURDER (Book #5)
LEFT TO ENVY (Book #6)
LEFT TO LAPSE (Book #7)
LEFT TO VANISH (Book #8)
LEFT TO HUNT (Book #9)
LEFT TO FEAR (Book #10)

THE AU PAIR SERIES
ALMOST GONE (Book#1)
ALMOST LOST (Book #2)
ALMOST DEAD (Book #3)

ZOE PRIME MYSTERY SERIES
FACE OF DEATH (Book#1)
FACE OF MURDER (Book #2)
FACE OF FEAR (Book #3)
FACE OF MADNESS (Book #4)
FACE OF FURY (Book #5)
FACE OF DARKNESS (Book #6)

A JESSIE HUNT PSYCHOLOGICAL SUSPENSE SERIES
THE PERFECT WIFE (Book #1)
THE PERFECT BLOCK (Book #2)
THE PERFECT HOUSE (Book #3)
THE PERFECT SMILE (Book #4)
THE PERFECT LIE (Book #5)
THE PERFECT LOOK (Book #6)
THE PERFECT AFFAIR (Book #7)
THE PERFECT ALIBI (Book #8)
THE PERFECT NEIGHBOR (Book #9)
THE PERFECT DISGUISE (Book #10)
THE PERFECT SECRET (Book #11)
THE PERFECT FAÇADE (Book #12)
THE PERFECT IMPRESSION (Book #13)
THE PERFECT DECEIT (Book #14)
THE PERFECT MISTRESS (Book #15)

ONCE TRAPPED (Book #13)
ONCE DORMANT (Book #14)
ONCE SHUNNED (Book #15)
ONCE MISSED (Book #16)
ONCE CHOSEN (Book #17)

MACKENZIE WHITE MYSTERY SERIES
BEFORE HE KILLS (Book #1)
BEFORE HE SEES (Book #2)
BEFORE HE COVETS (Book #3)
BEFORE HE TAKES (Book #4)
BEFORE HE NEEDS (Book #5)
BEFORE HE FEELS (Book #6)
BEFORE HE SINS (Book #7)
BEFORE HE HUNTS (Book #8)
BEFORE HE PREYS (Book #9)
BEFORE HE LONGS (Book #10)
BEFORE HE LAPSES (Book #11)
BEFORE HE ENVIES (Book #12)
BEFORE HE STALKS (Book #13)
BEFORE HE HARMS (Book #14)

AVERY BLACK MYSTERY SERIES
CAUSE TO KILL (Book #1)
CAUSE TO RUN (Book #2)
CAUSE TO HIDE (Book #3)
CAUSE TO FEAR (Book #4)
CAUSE TO SAVE (Book #5)
CAUSE TO DREAD (Book #6)

KERI LOCKE MYSTERY SERIES
A TRACE OF DEATH (Book #1)
A TRACE OF MUDER (Book #2)
A TRACE OF VICE (Book #3)
A TRACE OF CRIME (Book #4)
A TRACE OF HOPE (Book #5)

Made in the USA
Monee, IL
13 August 2024

63825649R10104